I0727299

THE HOUSEWIFE ASSASSIN'S HOLLYWOOD SCREAM PLAY

JOSIE BROWN

A BOOK BY

SIGNAL PRESS

ONE OF MANY GREAT SIGNAL PRESS BOOKS

San Francisco, CA

Library of Congress Cataloging-in-Publication Data is available upon request

Cover Design by Andrew Brown, ClickTwiceDesign.com

Digital Formatting by Austin Brown, CheapEbookFormatting.com

Trade Paperback ISBN: 978-1-942052-16-6

Hardcover ISBN: 978-1-942052-30-2

V022319

can't wait to read the next in the series. Highly Recommended!"

—*CrimeThrillerGirl.com*

"This was an addictive read–gritty but funny at the same time. I ended up reading it in just one evening and couldn't go to sleep until I knew what the outcome would be! It was action-packed and humorous from the start, and that continued throughout, I was pleased to discover that this is the first of a series and look forward to getting my hands on Book Two so I can see where life takes Donna and her family next!"

—*Me, My Books, and I*

"The two halves of Donna's life make sense. As you follow her story, there's no point where you think of her as "Assassin Donna" vs. "Mummy Donna', her attitude to life is even throughout. I really like how well this is done. And as for Jack. I'll have one of those, please?"

—*The Northern Witch's Book Blog*

Novels in The Housewife Assassin Series

The Housewife Assassin's Handbook (Book 1)

The Housewife Assassin's Guide to Gracious Killing (Book 2)

The Housewife Assassin's Killer Christmas Tips (Book 3)

The Housewife Assassin's Relationship Survival Guide (Book 4)

The Housewife Assassin's Vacation to Die For (Book 5)

The Housewife Assassin's Recipes for Disaster (Book 6)

The Housewife Assassin's Hollywood Scream Play (Book 7)

The Housewife Assassin's Killer App (Book 8)

The Housewife Assassin's Hostage Hosting Tips (Book 9)

The Housewife Assassin's Garden of Deadly Delights (Book 10)

The Housewife Assassin's Tips for Weddings, Weapons, and Warfare (Book 11)

The Housewife Assassin's Husband Hunting Hints (Book 12)

The Housewife Assassin's Ghost Protocol (Book 13)

The Housewife Assassin's Terrorist TV Guide (Book 14)

The Housewife Assassin's Deadly Dossier (Book 15: The Series Prequel)

The Housewife Assassin's Greatest Hits (Book 16)

The Housewife Assassin's Fourth Estate Sale (Book 17)

The Housewife Assassin's Horrorscope (Book 18)

The Mummy

> "You're wondering, 'What is a place like this doing in a girl like me?'"
>
> Rachel Weisz, as "Evelyn"

Go ahead, gentle reader, and admit it: you love being scared by things that go bump in the night.

It's why you spend hours watching thrillers and monster movies.

And why you've seen every Hitchcock film, and memorized each wry aside in every "Sherlock Holmes" episode.

All the more reason to put on your favorite Snuggie, clasp a comforting pillow to your heaving bosom, and huddle down into your sofa.

Word of caution: try not to get so caught up in the action that you shoot the idiot who keeps knocking on your front door! "He *should have waited until the commercial break," won't earn you an acquittal for justifiable homicide.*

I PAUSE, JUST A MOMENT, TO ADMIRE HIS BEAUTIFUL BACK—taut, coiled muscles under a wide expanse of shoulders.

The cool air makes him shiver. Or is it his anticipation?

It's rude of me to keep him waiting. If my mother taught me anything, it was to be prompt for every engagement, no matter how distasteful or obligatory.

So, off to work we go.

My mind's eye sees everything in real time, and in Technicolor. The first stroke of my whip hits him diagonally across his back. A welt rises, blanched of the blood beneath the skin—but only for a second. Then, a torrent of blood, the shade of deep rubies, flows from his open wound.

My prisoner flinches against the shackles that bind him to the basement wall. He groans, but he cannot scream. Otherwise, he'd choke on the ball gag clenched between his teeth.

He braces for the next lash.

The client paying me to put my prisoner in this position had one explicit demand: "Make it look real." But let me make this perfectly clear: *I take no joy in this task.* If you presume all assassins live to give pain, you're sorely mistaken.

So, to muddle through it, I fantasize that he's someone else.

In this case, I pretend that he is not Bernard Martin, the

French UN delegate who has been trading his country's secrets to the Russians, which has already cost six undercover agents their lives. And I am not the freelance assassin who has been hired by France's Central Directorate of Interior Intelligence to exterminate him while playing yet another dominatrix he has sought out for pain and pleasure and perhaps penance for crimes against his country.

For just a few more moments, I forget that I'm here to administer an injection of aconite, so as to leave the police with the theory that Monsieur Martin died of a fatal heart attack while being whipped into an orgiastic frenzy. The French government can shrug off a sex scandal. Better that Monsieur Martin betray his wife than his country.

To make this easier on both of us, I pretend he is my soon-to-be ex-husband, Carl Stone.

Now the strokes are fast and furious. In no time at all, his once beautiful back is crossed in a lattice of blood.

He gasps the mutually-agreed-upon safety phrase: *la douleur et la joie*. Get real! In truth, can pain ever be equated with joy?

When he realizes I'm ignoring his request to stop, his pleas get louder. My raucous laugh has Monsieur Martin frantic to break out of his restraints.

Good luck with that, dude.

Every lash gives him as much pain as Carl brought me. I ignore my prisoner's sobs, the same way Carl ignored me and his children during the five years I thought he was dead.

Change of plans, a voice whispers in my ear.

I ignore it, too. There is no turning back now.

Carl broke my heart. To make matters even worse, he's

been nominated by our new president to the post of US Director of Intelligence, which will put him in charge of all sixteen US Department of Defense agencies dealing with domestic and international intel gathering. He's already made it very clear that all NSA contracts are on the chopping block. The first to go will be the one that my employer— Acme Industries—has with the CIA; he wants to break my spirit, too.

In return, I'm breaking his back.

Make that an aortic vessel. The spasm has my prisoner convulsing. His eyes roll back in his head and he slumps down, despite being held against the wall by his shackles.

"What the hell are you doing?" the voice asks me.

Suddenly, I realize it's not my conscience, but Jack Craig, my mission leader, talking to me through my ear bud. He is also my soul mate, and the reason I want Carl out of my life, once and for all.

You know what they say: two's company, three's a crowd. Especially if the third one is a psychopathic terrorist.

To cover my guilt, I fake annoyance. "What do you think I'm doing? I'm making it 'look real.'"

"Didn't you hear me?" Jack shouts. "There's been a change in plans. We've picked up the wrong guy. It wasn't supposed to be Bernard Martin, but *Martin Bernard*. Unfortunately for us, both guys are into BDSM, which is why we intercepted the wrong French diplomat's call. In fact, Martin —the one with that as his first name—is a top."

Oh, mon Dieu!

I fumble in the décolleté of my patent leather teddy for the key to his shackles. Unfortunately, it's fallen below my breasts. Damn it, I knew I should have sewn bra cups into this getup! I'm so jam-packed in the damn thing that by the time I fish it out from my nether regions and unlock his bindings, he's already foaming at the mouth. No amount of chest pounding, mouth-to-mouth resuscitation, or guilty prayers will bring him back.

"What's the prognosis?" Jack asks.

I wince. "Let's just say First Name Bernard *mange les pissenlits par la racine.*"

"'Eating the dandelions from the root up?'" After a long silence, he sighs. "*Merde.* We can break the news to Ryan later. Hightail it back to the van. We've got only twenty minutes to make it to the office for a meet-and-greet with a new triple-A-rated client."

The rating indicates a client with security clearance from a foreign government. "Shouldn't I go home and change first?"

"Nope, sorry. Time is of the essence. The client is wheels-up in an hour—with or without us. But he'll be leaving with some lucky black-ops team, even if it's not one of Acme's."

It had better be us. To stay in the good graces of our new president, Lee Chiffray, Acme needs to rack up as many brownie points as possible.

I stare down at the body at my feet. *If only it were the real Carl.*

Rigor mortis is setting in, but I'm still able to maneuver Monsieur Martin's hands over his private parts before heading out the door.

It's the least I can do for him.

"YOUR SERVICES COME HIGHLY RECOMMENDED," CROWN PRINCE Sheikh Hamdan bin Al Mubarak assures my boss, Ryan Clancy, all the while undressing me with his eyes.

I shift uncomfortably in my chair, and not just because there's nothing but a thin strand of patent leather ass floss between me and the cold metal seat.

"We aim to please." Ryan Clancy's smile is tepid at best.

"Al Mubarak, you say? Perhaps of the Abu Dhabi Mubaraks?" Another of Acme's agents, Dominic Fleming, taps his lips with a forefinger, an obvious sign of contemplation. "I say, old boy, I think your brother was in my house, at Eton—Baldwin's Bec!" He holds his hand an inch above his head. "Somewhat taller, eh? Dapper dresser, and a jammy bugger at cribbage?"

Ryan's glare does nothing to deter Dominic's gaze. The last thing Acme needs is Dominic chasing off a potential client with a snotty little game of *Who Are You and Why Should I Give a Damn.*

The sheikh smirks. "I think not. Our kingdom, Umm al-Quwain, is the smallest of the seven sovereign emirate states. And my father preferred Gordonstoun for his sons' preparatory education. Then again, who knows? I am only the fourteenth son of twenty-three, and sadly, not all of us have lived up to our potential."

Snap.

I've got to give Dominic credit, his nostrils flair, but his smile stays put.

"Your eminence, you say this mission would entail

securing an antiquity from an archaeological dig in Yemen?" Ryan moves so that he blocks the sheikh's view of Dominic. I wish he'd block me, too, what with the way the prince is staring at me.

"That is correct." The sheikh nods. He takes a sip from his teacup. "It was raided by Al Qaeda, just two days ago. The archeologists hailed from Canada. They had just uncovered ancient ruins in Yemen's desert region, Ramlat al-Sab`atayn. It is about forty-five kilometers from one of Yemen's ancient cities, Sana'a—or, as it is called in the Christian *Bible*, Sheba." With a flick of his wrist, he waves away our stares. "After interpreting petroglyphs on two large pillars at the entry of the ruin, the archeologists realized they had discovered the tomb of Bilqis."

Arnie Locklear, our mission team's tech op, gives a low whistle. "Do you mean the burial site of the *actual* Queen of Sheba? It would date back to, what, 980 BCE or something?"

The prince nods. "You know your *Bible*, young man. Our *Quran* also notes that the queen—Bilqis—sought out King Solomon for his wisdom and, in turn, learned to put her faith not in false idols, but in the one true God—Allah."

"Have the tomb's antiquities been secured?"

"Unfortunately, no. But there is only one way to secure entry, via a secret panel. It is our great luck that the Al Qaeda raiders have been unable to find it—thus far." The prince pulls a handkerchief from his jacket pocket in order to wipe the monocle he wears over his right eye. "The tomb holds the queen's sarcophagus. In her hands, she holds a jewel-encrusted scepter."

Everyone leans forward, intrigued. Yep, that has certainly got our full attention.

"Around its staff are petroglyphs detailing her meeting with King Solomon." The prince pauses as he bows his head. "Just at the moment of the scepter's discovery, the rebels swarmed the site. Sadly, only one member of the excavation crew, a woman, was in the tomb, and survived the rebels' attack. The rest of her party were slaughtered. Frightened—for obvious reasons, considering her knowledge of Al Qaeda's torture techniques—she waited until nightfall before re-emerging and making her way back to Sana'a. Afraid she might run into the rebels again, she had the foresight to leave the scepter in the queen's tomb. As you can imagine, it is priceless. All the more reason it must be retrieved before the rebels learn of its existence."

"At this point, you presume the raiders have given up, and we can waltz right in?" Jack asks.

The sheikh shrugged. "I don't expect it will be that easy. However, your government's satellites show little interest from the raiders. Their own search of the surrounding ruins revealed a few minor antiquities, nothing more." His eyes swept over me. "Besides, most of the region's villages have already been decimated, or the tribal sheikhs in control have been paid off. The rebels have, as you Americans so quaintly put it, bigger fish to fry. They have moved onto the task of terrorizing Yemen's larger cities." His eyes graze over me as he massages the word, "terrorize."

"Then it should be safe enough for your own security teams to secure the ruins and the treasure you know is there," Jack reasons.

"Our neighbor to the south would not welcome Saudi Arabian armed forces within its borders."

"And yet, Yemen's tribal chiefs accept your, er, 'financial patronage' with open arms. Or, I should say, palms. Go figure," mutters another of our usual mission members, Abu Nagashahi.

"Until now." The prince's nod is proffered with a sneer at our Persian associate. "These days, Al Qaeda's pockets are also lined with gold. And sadly, Yemen's tribal fiefdoms are always up for bid. All the more reason the Emirates—and the United States, for that matter—must bolster the current Yemeni president's administration, and in this case, his cultural minister's attempts to protect what is left of their country's priceless artifacts. In the long run, they may be what save it."

"That, and its oil," Arnie Locklear, our mission's tech op, murmurs.

The prince frowns. "Al Qaeda is also sabotaging Yemen's pipelines, almost on a daily basis. But terrorism is just one of several factors which has led those of us who rule the Middle East to face up to the fact that, whereas oil ruled our past and present, it may play a diminished role in our future."

This is an intriguing comment, coming from someone whose family has made billions of dollars from black gold.

As if reading my mind, the prince adds, "Now that China has crossed the bridge into the twenty-first century, it is faced with the cons as well as the pros of a modern society. Its air can't stay black and still have its citizens survive. GDP is meaningless if you have no citizens to enjoy it. When the

Chinese finally put an anti-pollution mandate in place, the rest of us will be forced to do the same." He frowns. "But the more immediate issue for my neighbor to the South is the protection of its most valuable asset—the scepter of Sheba."

"Yemen is a very important ally of our country—as are all the Arab Emirate states, Umm al-Quwain included. All the more reason we're ready to send in our number one team," Ryan assures him. "At your behest, they'll leave tonight." The sheikh's country may be tiny, but it's a financial cash cow to several US petrochemical corporations. With US government contracts drying up, Acme has no option but to accept the mission.

So yes, our success would be a feather in Acme's cap.

The sheikh nods toward me. "She is also on this 'number one team?'"

I understand why Ryan hesitates before answering. In the sheikh's world, women rarely do a man's job, let alone a deadly one. "Donna is one of our most capable agents."

The prince motions for me to stand up. I rise slowly, unsure of what else he expects from me. He circles me, as if I were a prized calf. If he opens my mouth to inspect my teeth, trust me, he'll lose a thumb.

Instead, he pulls a retractable measuring tape out of his jacket pocket—

And stretches it around my breasts, shoulders and back.

What...the....

The next thing I know, he has the damn thing around my hips, bending slightly, to read my measurement. "*Hmmm.* It will be a tight squeeze, but she'll do."

Jack puts a hand on my shoulder, and just in time. Otherwise, my knee would have slammed into the prince's monocle, and he'd have to find an eye patch to match his headscarf.

Still deep in thought, he murmurs, "Excuse my impertinence, but it is necessary to indulge me. You see, in order to enter the tomb, someone with a small build will have to slip through a compartment with an opening no bigger than eighteen by eight inches. Your measurements fit the bill—but barely."

Suddenly, the heads of everyone else in the room swivel in my direction, then tilt in order to follow his stare:

Which is aimed at my bum.

By the looks on their faces, I know what they're thinking.

In response, I scratch my nose with my middle finger.

As for you, Lovely Reader, I know what you're thinking, too: *Poor Donna! Has it come to this—?*

Tomb robbing?

No.

Well, not exactly. I wouldn't do anything if it weren't government-sanctioned, now would I?

Okay, maybe.

But this ain't one of those times. However, these are the times that try spies' souls, what with the NSA cancelling black-ops contracts left and right.

Should Carl be put in charge, my neck will certainly be on the chopping block.

Maybe the prince should have measured it, too.

By the time we land in the Yemeni desert, it is just an hour before dawn.

Besides blowing up pipelines built by US and Canadian oil companies, for almost a week now Al Qaeda has been detonating car bombs all over Yemen's larger cities—the capitol, Sana'a, and Amanat Al Asimah.

For all we know, it's already too late, and Bilqis' tomb has also been blown to smithereens.

This is a three-man mission—just Jack, Acme's pilot George Taylor, and me. So as not to attract the attention of either the rebels or the local police, George flew our Super Puma helicopter from a Saudi Arabian airstrip just across the Yemeni border, touching down four miles from the GPS coordinates of the dig site, which is in a remote canyon. The Puma's cargo hold also contains three motorcycles, on the off chance our getaway has to be made on land instead.

While Jack oversees all satellite reconnaissance within a forty-mile range of the dig, I'm to go in alone, via motorcycle.

An hour before we landed, Al Qaeda set off a bomb at a major shopping mall in Sana'a. Thank goodness, Yemeni police squads are too busy herding fleeing citizens through security checkpoints to notice a lone biker zipping through the desert on a starry night.

So that I don't unwittingly run into roving bands of Al Qaeda Shi'a, I'm riding without a headlight. To compensate, I wear infrared night vision goggles under my helmet.

I keep my eye on the digital GPS system of my Super-moto as I parallel the road, and I zigzag through the desert at the first sign of lights in any direction. For this journey,

I'm not in regional garb—a headscarf to cover all but my eyes, and a floor-length *abaya*, both made of plain white linen. Instead, I wear a bike helmet with a tinted visor and a bulky black leather jumpsuit that obscures my womanly curves.

Better to be shot as an enemy than raped as a victim.

For that matter, the marauders have plenty of others to traumatize during the chaos. By staying off-road, I've barely sidestepped a group of livestock-herding Bedouin women, heading south.

But just a mile behind them is a car, commandeered by two men. The one in the passenger seat shoots an Uzi skyward, just for the hell of it. At the speed at which they're traveling, they'll catch up with the women in no time. What will take place won't be pretty, and unfortunately, the memories will stay with the women forever—

That is, if they're allowed to live.

I turn my motorcycle in the direction of the car.

Because my GPS coordinates are being tracked by Jack through my contact lenses and ear buds—which also give him wireless feeds of everything I see and hear—I'm not at all surprised to hear him warn me, "Donna, you don't have time for a detour. It'll be daylight soon. We've got exactly one hour to pull off this mission and turn the plane around."

He's right. Stopping to help them will set me back badly. But it will haunt me for the rest of my life if I don't do something, so I circle back around.

When I finally spot the rebels' car on the side of the road, I turn off my engine. So that they don't hear me, I jog the last quarter of a mile.

I get there just in time to see the driver yank the youngest —a girl of about thirteen—out from the cluster of frightened women, and drag her behind his car while his compatriot holds her screaming mother and aunts at bay with his Uzi.

The man has already shoved his pants to his ankles with one hand and is holding the sobbing, struggling girl down with the other when I come up behind him.

When my switchblade slices the rapist's throat, he lets out a groan, more painful than orgasmic.

Every time I take a life, I'm awed and humbled by the act: the stark fear glazing my victims' eyes, that final gasp of realization, followed by the peaceful calm of resignation; then, finally, the anticipation of oblivion.

Will I feel the same, when my time comes?

The young girl's hysterical screams are so loud that, by the time I get to the other man, all it takes to finish him off is a single shot to the back of his head with the rapist's handgun.

As the women bless me to Allah, I toss the gun at the girl's mother, along with the ammo cache that I found in the back of the rebels' car. "God's gift is not me, but your own lives. Keep moving," I command them.

Then I dart back out into the dark desert night.

I have no doubt they'll make it. The mother smiled when what was left of her captor's head hit the sandy asphalt.

I would have reached my destination quicker, but a skirmish between some tribe and another band of marauders forces me to loop out so far from the target coordinates that it takes me another twenty minutes to get back on course.

When, finally, I enter the narrow mouth of the canyon, I

yank off my helmet and scan the valley before me for anything that resembles an excavation.

Then I see it: the ruins surrounding Bilqis' tomb.

In the dawn's early light, the outline of the ancient mounds resemble a sleeping old woman, fatigued and limbs akimbo. For the past three millennia, the hot breath of the desert has been blowing sheets of sand against her crumbling flanks.

Silence shrouds every corner of the ruins. Good, I'm alone. But just in case someone else comes calling while I'm inside, I hide my bike behind a copse of scrub trees.

Now that two thousand years of dust has been moved from a hole some sixty feet wide and 100 feet deep, a massive tomb, built on the backs of a thousand Sabaean slaves, is nakedly exposed.

Wraiths of dust, caught in the dawn's early light, waltz lazily around the clay pillars flanking its entrance. Carved onto each is a likeness of the queen of Sheba. On one, the canes she holds in each of her hands are topped with the heads of lions. Her straight-on stare is blank, her eyes filled solid with clay.

On the other pillar, Bilqis is in profile. Her eye—a slit, really—is dark, fathomless.

I take a switchblade from the back of my boot. Following our client's instructions, I stab the empty-eyed silhouette once, quickly and deeply.

When the blade connects with a clasp buried deep within the eyehole, a tiny trap door at my feet slides open. It's just large enough for me to drop down into it.

Okay, no. My shoulders are stuck.

"What's taking so long?" The impatience in Jack's voice is enough incentive to shift my arms. They are squeezing my breasts to the point that I've given myself the kind of cleavage I've only dreamed of. *Hmmm.* I should pose like this more often—

And that does the trick. I fall through the opening—

Onto some sort of slide that takes me on a ride in pitch darkness.

Finally, I skid to a stop. With trembling hands, I flick on my flashlight. The shadows swallow its glow. Still, I angle its beam around the room. Despite its massive size, the room is empty, except for a rectangular stone box—six feet in width, three feet in depth, and only three feet wide.

"The queen of Sheba's sarcophagus!" Jack's awed whisper echoes in my ear.

The lid has been nudged to one side, but only by a few inches.

I take a deep breath as I give it a shove. It is hinged in such a way that it slides open easily—not with a creak, but with a whisper.

The body inside is tiny, almost childlike. It is wrapped in weathered strips of cloth.

The scepter is clutched in her sheathed hands.

I shudder. Jack must see my head shaking because he says, "I know this sounds callous, but if we're going to get out of here anytime soon, you're just going to have to go for it."

"I know." Still, I feel creepy.

Like a grave robber.

I try to uncoil Bilqis' stiffened fingers from the scepter,

but she won't let go. Soon I'm in a wrestling match with her. To give myself some leverage, I step up on the ledge of the pedestal beneath the sarcophagus, grab the scepter with both hands, and jerk it back, as hard and as fast as I can.

I've torn it loose.

But one of her hands is still clutching it.

Gently, I pull it off, and place it back on her chest.

I swear, I don't like the way she's staring at me.

The roar of engines breaks our gal pal moment. By the way the sound echoes through the tomb, I can tell it's a large fleet.

"Jack, what's going on outside?"

"You've got company. I'm opening the satellite feed into your right contact lens, so that you can see for yourself," Jack tells me.

What I see doesn't make me happy. The motorcade has stopped just outside the entrance of the tomb, kicking up a cloud of fine desert silt. By the time it drifts away, several rebels, dusted from head to toe in shimmering dirt, have already sprung to the ground. They are crouching warily beside their vehicles, listening intently for any wayward sounds.

Finally, one motions the all-clear. Squinting through the sights of their Uzis, the rebels fan out in all directions.

Two of the men head to the front of the tomb. One of them, the taller of the two, runs his hands along the face of the front wall. The other, short and with a hook in his nose, angrily smacks the wall with the butt of this rifle.

Yeah, good luck with that, buddy.

Frustrated, Shorty shoots his rifle, then ducks as bullets

ricochet off the wall and one of the two large columns. Tall Guy literally slams into the other column to avoid a stray.

The column topples over onto the tomb. The building shakes as the wall caves in, exposing an antechamber.

Now they are one thin wall away from me.

"Where the hell am I supposed to hide?" I mutter frantically. "It's not like 1 can climb back up the damn rabbit hole that put me here!"

"Jump into the sarcophagus!" Jack commands me.

"What? Are you crazy?"

But he's right. It's the only place to hide.

I run to it and jump in—

Beside Bilqis.

In order to fit, I've got to hug her, John and Yoko-style.

Before taking the position, I shift the lid so that it looks as if it's closed. In fact, it's angled in such a way that I can peek out through a slim crack. If I'm lucky, they won't bother to lift it up.

Two men are now standing there in the doorway, haloed in the hazy sunlight. They look around. The emptiness of the room disappoints them, I'm sure. Tall Dude seems afraid to step inside, but Shorty circles the sarcophagus. His slow, steady footsteps echo off the high arched walls of the ancient tomb.

He leans against the sarcophagus and lights a cigarette, as if he has all the time in the world.

My mind warns me not to breathe, not to move, not to make a sound.

Finally, he shrugs and starts out.

He's just reached the threshold when I sneeze.

His head whips in my direction. His eyes turn toward the sarcophagus.

I am so screwed.

He starts over, but Tall Dude, whose eyes are open wide with fear, grabs his arm. When Shorty shakes it off, the other pleads with him, in Arabic. I don't know what they're saying, but whatever it is won't buy me much time.

"Donna, there's something funny about the sarcophagus' dimensions," Jack mutters. "The surveillance feed on you is reading a spatial anomaly."

"What the hell are you talking about?" I whisper back.

"I'm trying to tell you that it's reading much deeper than it should, considering the mass of the sarcophagus' base. My guess is that it has a false bottom."

"Why, pray tell?"

"If you remember, those preparing the royals for the afterlife were sometimes buried alive with them. A false bottom would have allowed the survivors to escape some-how. If so, there's got to be some sort of lever to open it. Start searching for it! I'm already on my way to you."

"Are you crazy? Stay put! One of us has to get out of here alive." For my children's sake, if for no other reason. We both know it. This is not the way I want them to learn that Jack—the only father they've ever known—has no legal rights to protect them from Carl, their biological father—

And the man who deserted all of us.

If Jack is right and there is a lever, I'd better find it quickly because Shorty seems to have won the argument. The men are moving toward the sarcophagus, guns ready.

I run my hand along the sides of the box, but I don't feel

anything. Finally I get the nerve to nudge Bilqis to one side. Beneath her is a carving of what seems to be a constellation made of diamonds. Venus is the largest stone. I smack it with my fist—

Just in time, too, because the lid is shoved to one side. The men are staring down at me.

But they're too late. Bilqis, the scepter and I drop through a trap door.

As I fall, Shorty's arm grabs for me—

And gets caught as the stone door slams shut again.

His blood-curdling scream follows me as I fly down the smooth stone chute.

So does his severed arm.

The ideal landing would have been a soft bed of hay, but hey, three thousand years has eliminated that option. There isn't even a fine powder to break my fall—

Just Bilqis, God bless the old girl.

I grab the scepter and jump to my feet. My flashlight reveals a long, dark tunnel. I take off at a trot, running for at least a mile.

At the end of the tunnel are a few crude stone steps. I search the walls for a lever. When I find it, a panel slides open just above them. As I run up the staircase, I'm hit with a whirlwind of centuries-old dust.

Jack is waiting for me topside.

"You've got to love GPS," he says with a smile.

I'm still coughing when he kisses me. When we pull away, his lips are caked in dust, too. The longer we laugh, the harder I cough.

We hop onto his motorcycle, and we're off.

CROWN PRINCE SHEIKH HAMDAN BIN AL MUBARAK IS THERE to meet the helicopter when it lands within Umm al-Quwain's border. I know I look like hell. My jumpsuit is shredded at the knees and elbows. Every time I shake my head, I shower myself in dirt.

The prince doesn't notice. He doesn't even look at me. He only has eyes for the scepter. He grabs it out of my hand and walks off, then waves us away, as if we've handed him a bowling trophy or something.

"You're welcome," I yell after him.

As the prince's limousine roars off into the desert, Jack says, "I don't think he caught your sarcasm."

"Hey, as long as he puts in a good word for Acme with our new president." I can't bring myself to call our former neighbor and new POTUS, Lee Chiffray, by his new title.

George is yelling at us from the cockpit of the helicopter, but because of the din of the Puma's engine, we only catch a few words—something about "Dominic" and "urgent."

We jump onboard and grab the satellite phone from him.

"Donna, my dear, tell me you've still got the scepter." There is no urgency in Dominic's voice. He might as well be asking about the weather.

"I'm pleased to announce that it's safely in the prince's hands. Why do you ask?"

"Ah! Pity."

Despite a desert temperature of over a hundred degrees, a cold dread washes over me. "I beg your pardon?"

"Turns out the prince isn't the fourteenth son of King Al Mubarak, after all. He isn't even the twenty-third."

I slump to the floor of the helicopter. "Are you saying he's—a fraud?"

"Afraid so, my dear. On a hunch, I rang up Brolly—he's the fifth son, you may recall me saying. A rather curious nickname, but it certainly fit the bill, since the old boy never remembered his umbrella, even in the dead of winter—"

"I don't care about this Brolly person! Get to the point, Dominic!"

"Yes, well, as I was saying, I felt that the fifth son certainly trumped the fourteenth, at least when it comes to something as important as prep schools," he chuckles. "As I suspected, the Al Mubaraks are Etonians, to a son. According to the fingerprints Arnie found on your mystery man's teacup, his real name is Freddie Mansour, and he originally hails from Chicago. His Interpol file reads like the script for *The Thomas Crown Affair*, what with the number of antiquities he's absconded with over the years."

"So, what you're telling me is that we stole a state treasure from a geo-politically strategic ally—*for a known antiquities thief to fence?*"

"Seems to be the case, yes."

"But—but we were told he had a Triple A client rating! That means he was thoroughly vetted and referred by the CIA!"

"Ah, there you go! As soon as Ryan realizes our largest client cocked it up, I'm sure you'll be off the hook." He doesn't sound too convincing. "As for Monsieur Bernard... well, dearie, if you blame that one on the cousins, you'll be sure to start an argy-bargy. Not to worry, we'll keep it our little secret from the boss man, until you choose to do otherwise."

"You mean, Ryan doesn't know about it yet?" Dominic is such a coward.

"Far be it from me to steal your thunder! Besides, he's already on his way to DC—to testify at the senate hearing for Carl's nomination. By the way, you and Jack are to meet him there, *tout de suite*."

Stunned, I hang up.

"What's up with Baron Blowhard?" Jack asks.

I pause, at a loss for how to answer him. If Jack is called to testify, I don't know what he'll say. I only hope that, whatever it is, it won't be the end of Acme.

Or the end of us, no matter what Carl has in store.

2

Advise and Consent

"Son, this is a Washington, DC kind of lie. It's when the other person knows you're lying, and also knows you know he knows."

Henry Fonda, as "Robert Leffingwell"

[FROM THE FIRST DRAFT OF THE SCREENPLAY FOR *THE Housewife Assassin's Handbook*]

FADE IN ON

INT. Senate Office Building Hearing Room — Day.

CARL STONE, a handsome and dapper man in his early forties, sits at a TABLE across from THE FIFTEEN SENATORS who make up the US SENATE SELECT COMMITTEE ON INTELLIGENCE.

Behind him, in the HEARING ROOM GALLERY sits a crowd of REPORTERS, PUBLIC ONLOOKERS, and SENATE AIDES.

Carl smiles slightly. He raps his fingers on the table to a sound only he can hear, as if he doesn't have a care in the world. All the while, he keeps his eyes firmly on the committee's YOUNGEST SENATOR, who is angrily reciting a litany of Carl's not-so-random acts of terror.

COMMITTEE CHAIRPERSON
*Senator, this is a nomination hearing, not a filibuster!
Unless you have proof of these allegations against Carl Stone, I'll have to
ask you to discontinue this line of questioning.*

YOUNGEST SENATOR
*In fact, I do have a witness who can validate these facts.
I'd like to call Mrs. Donna Stone to the witness stand.*

SFX: CREAKING DOOR, from the rear of the room. Then the STEADY CLICK OF HEELS on the MARBLE FLOOR.

All heads turn as DONNA STONE—slim, stunningly beautiful, and dressed chicly in designer couture—makes her way to the WITNESS STAND.

ANGLE ON Carl, who has also craned his neck in her direction. His smile fades. His eyes open wide, as if he's seen a ghost.

DONNA
(murmuring as she saunters past him:)
Welcome to hell, darling.

(CONT.)

THE DUTY-FREE SHOP WITHIN DC'S CLOSEST PRIVATE AIRPORT— Manassas—is a joke. The only clothes I'm able to purchase before hightailing it over to the Senate building for Carl's nomination hearing are Day-Glo sneakers, drawstring track pants for a fat man, and a tee-shirt that reads:

THE ONLY DIFFERENCE
BETWEEN CONGRESS AND THE MAFIA
IS THAT ONE OF THEM IS *ORGANIZED*.

At least I was able to wash most of the desert dust out of my hair in the ladies' room sink. But even after running it under the hand dryer a couple of times, I'm still quite a fright. Perhaps if I pull my hair back with a scrunchie I won't look too scary to the members of the Senate Intelligence Committee.

Jack must feel the same way because he winces as I exit the ladies' room. "Just my opinion, but I doubt that get-up will help you win friends, let alone influence a senate nomination panel."

I shrug. "It was either this, or buy the 1970s Braniff stewardess uniform from the airport's museum."

"Then you've made the right choice. No need to give anyone on that committee a Mile High Club flashback, on the off-chance that his or her spouse is sitting in the gallery."

Since Yemen, Jack and I have avoided the topic of what either of us will say, if, in fact, we have to take the stand and swear on a stack of Bibles as to what we know about Carl's actions. I guess there's no better time to discuss it than now, since we have an hour's worth of Route 66 and I-395 traffic ahead of us.

"If either of us should be called upon to testify, I presume the best tactic is to keep all worms in their cans." I don't look at him as I speak. Instead, I fix my face with my duty-free treasure trove of Cover Girl products. "You know, answer the senators' questions with as few words as possible. Keep on point, and—well, stay away from anything that might be misconstrued as a possible breach of conduct on our part."

"This, coming from someone whose tee-shirt may actually have her pegged as a hostile witness." He sighs. "If what you're asking is whether or not I plan on jeopardizing Acme, and for that matter, our livelihood, I think you know the answer to that. But, at the same time, I'll do my best to make sure that Carl's nomination does not get approved. If anything, they should know the truth about him, and hang him for being a traitor."

He reads the long pause between us as fear on my part.

Good—because that's exactly what it is.

Just in case he's forgotten, I gently remind him, "You know, you can always plead the fifth. Alan Swan says—"

"Alan Swan?" Jack busts out laughing. "You actually talked to that dufus of a divorce lawyer about this?"

Now I feel guilty about my panicked cell phone call from the ladies' room. "I felt it prudent that one of us talk to someone! Acme's directives to its agents may have been government-sanctioned, but you've got to admit, there have been quite a few off-the-books indiscretions. Besides, it's not as if Ryan has gone out of his way to prep us for this stuff."

"Don't blame Ryan. These last few weeks he's had his hands full, reminding our clients of all our good deeds on their behalf."

I wipe away a tear. "I don't. I blame myself. If only I'd killed Carl when I had the opportunity."

My chance came after Carl resurfaced—to me, alone—after five years being presumed dead. I shot at him when he tried to set off a deadly nanobomb in a stadium—one that would have been fatal to tens of thousands of mothers, fathers, and children, including ours.

I should have aimed for his head, but my heart got the better of me. Instead, I wounded him.

He escaped, killing two men in the process.

Jack shrugs. "If anyone is at fault, it's me. I had a chance to take him out, too. Remember? If I had, we wouldn't be in this predicament."

Jack had been chasing after the Quorum even during the years I'd presumed Carl was dead. He had been the first Acme operative to suspect Carl was a double agent—after Carl coerced Jack's wife, Valentina, to abscond with a microdot containing the code to the DaaS Cloud holding Acme's worldwide directory of agents and assets.

By the time he'd caught up with Carl, he'd already fallen in love with me.

Six months after Carl escaped, Jack caught up to him. But he also hesitated to shoot him—because he felt that the act of killing Carl, the father of my children, would always stand between us.

Was he right?

Now, almost two years later, we both know the answers that eluded us then.

Yes, I'm over Carl.

And yes, it's time to take him down.

We must not fail to convince those who can approve his nomination that he's the biggest threat to US national security.

It's not just our jobs at stake, but our lives.

Jack takes my hands in his and looks me in the eye. "Donna, both of us must tell the truth—not just because lying would perjure us, but because we have nothing to fear. The former intelligence director sanctioned every one of our missions. That being said, we'll answer the committee's questions within the boundaries of our missions' security classifications."

"By doing so, will we be able to stop Carl's appointment?"

He rolls his forefinger from my palm to the crook of my elbow, where he lets it linger.

I'm always in awe of his tenderness.

"If he's confirmed anyway, at least we will have done our best to put his actions on the record—without incriminating ourselves," he continues, "and then let the chips fall where they may."

It's my personal mission to make sure they don't land on Jack.

Otherwise, they will cost Carl dearly.

BY THE TIME WE GET TO THE SENATE BUILDING, THE HEARING IS already in session. The public gallery in the hearing room is chock-full of those whose livelihoods depend on securing a contract with any one of the sixteen elements of the US intelligence community, or the IC as it calls itself.

Besides the Central Intelligence Agency (CIA), there is a veritable alphabet soup of federal bureaus. The Department of Defense comes to the party with the largest posse, which includes the National Reconnaissance Office (NRO), the National Geospatial-Intelligence Agency (NGA), the National Security Agency (NSA), the Army Intelligence and Security Command (INSCOM), and the Drug Enforcement Administration (DEA).

There is also the Department of Energy's Office of Intelligence and Counterintelligence (OICI), as well as the Treasury Department's Office of Terrorism and Financial Intelligence (TFI). The State Department's Bureau of Intelligence and Research (INR) is its liaison to this motley crew.

Etcetera, etcetera, etcetera.

The heads of all of these departments are here today. Frowny faces all around. I imagine there are a few sweaty palms as well. If not through personal experience, then certainly their own reconnaissance has made them well aware of Carl's reputation as a rogue black-ops agent, a terrorist, and a man bent on revenge.

Welcome to my world, boys.

Have they been back-channeling what they know to the nominating committee? Do they understand that telling the truth is the only thing that will take him down, or will they play ball to save their own covert operations?

I pray the former, but if I had to bet, I'd put my chips on the latter.

Apparently the Senate Select Subcommittee on Intelligence's chairman, Senator Vanna Ackerman, has already made her opening remarks because Carl is beginning his introductory statement:

"When President Chiffray asked me to be Director of National Intelligence, he made it emphatically clear that he wants someone who can build the intelligence community into an integrated team. He wants someone who will tell policymakers what they need to know, even if it isn't what they want to hear. Lastly, he wants someone who knows how to get things done in a bipartisan, professional manner." Carl's arms open wide, as if he's embracing the entire committee. "I am humbled by his nomination. Should I be confirmed, I will serve diligently and competently."

Throughout his spiel, Senator Ackerman's face has been frozen in an implacable stare. This moderate statesperson, who hails from a state as purple as her ill-fitting Armani suit, is known for being blunt in front of the press and a take-no-prisoners negotiator behind the Senate's heavy oak closed doors, all of which bodes well for Team Acme.

Um…wait a minute. Maybe not. Suddenly there is a twinkle in her eyes. Her lips lift into a provocative come-hither smile.

Oh my God…

She's flirting with Carl.

Proof is in the way she broaches her very first question —*while toying with the string of pearls around her neck.* "You've proudly served your country as a US Marine, have you not, Lieutenant Stone?"

Carl's Mona Lisa smile is a show of modesty. "Yes, that's correct, Senator. I feel my experience in the military – starting with my two tours of active duty – provided a wealth of experience in intelligence, which has been expanded and honed by the things I've done since retiring from military service."

A loud sneeze, coming from the other side of the room, barely disguises the word, "Bullshit!"

I'll say.

It sounded a lot like Arnie, but if he's here, he's in disguise, which wouldn't surprise me in the least. This sort of function is catnip to him, custom-made to be crashed.

Senator Ackerman scowls as she cranes her neck in order to take in the public gallery. "For those who wish to comment extemporaneously, let there be no doubt that you will be escorted out of the room posthaste. Do I make myself clear?"

Silence.

Ryan's eyes seek out mine. He frowns.

I shake my head to assure him that it wasn't me.

However, if Carl topples over from a knife in his back, I'll gladly take the fall.

But they'll have to catch me first.

Having chastised the crowd, Senator Ackerman shuffles the papers in front of her. The first two buttons of her blouse are undone so that when she leans forward, she creates a deep chasm between her breasts. "And as I recall, Lieutenant Stone, you're also a decorated veteran."

"Yes, Madame Chairman. A Silver Star, and the Distinguished Flying Cross."

She tilts her head to one side, as if she's heard the whisper of an angel. "Such a brave man," she rhapsodizes. "I can see why the president feels as strongly as he does about your abilities. That said, I'll cede the floor to the committee's vice chairman, Senator C. Bright Kuley."

Senator Kuley, a Republican who hails from the great state of Missouri, is one of the country's venerable senior statesmen. Besides being the ranking minority leader on this committee and his party's whip, in his six terms in the Senate he has previously served as chairman of the Judiciary, Foreign, and Homeland Security and Governmental Affairs committees.

He's been married to the same woman for forty years. Together, they have three grown children, and eight grandchildren. Nary a scandal has sullied his long tenure, hence his nickname, "Bright the White Knight."

Kuley frowns as he positions the microphone in front of him. I tense up. Will he, too, be lobbing softballs for Carl to hit out of the park?

"Despite your stellar service record, *Mister* Stone, your most recent activities were in the private sector, were they not?"

Carl nods. "Yes, Mr. Vice Chairman. I was also an independent contractor with a company that holds contracts with at least twelve of the intelligence community's organizations—"

"'Independent contractor?' More like rogue agent," I mutter to Jack.

"Shhh," he warns me. "Don't get us kicked out of here."

"—and this gave me great insight into their roles, as well as the strengths and limitations, of contractors," Carl continues. "I also know how the IC is viewed from the outside, and how financial goals motivate a commercial entity as it competes for, wins, and fulfills contracts."

"Even to the point of creating the terror it claims to stamp out, is that not so, Mr. Stone?"

Carl nods, ever so innocently. "You're absolutely correct, sir."

"In fact, Mr. Stone, your actions as an operative in—and some would say *leader* of the terrorist organization known as the Quorum put you on the World's Most Wanted Fugitives List for at least two years. Now I ask you, in what alternative universe would you, let alone our new president, envision a known terrorist as the US Director of Intelligence?"

I clench Jack's hand in mine. *Finally, someone is going to nail him to the cross I've been bearing for the past seven years!*

Carl's smile doesn't waver. Instead, he eases against the back of his chair, as if enjoying a polite conversation with an old friend as opposed to one of the most powerful men in the country. "I have heard expressions of concern about my independent status. The truth of the matter is that, while under deep cover, I infiltrated one of the most notorious terrorist organizations—*and brought it to its knees.*"

A gasp is heard through the room—

—Only to be drowned out by my exclamation, "Bullshit! Yo Carl, stop me if I'm wrong, but wasn't it you who tried to set off a nanobomb in a stadium filled with people? And weren't you the lunatic who almost shot down POTUS with a heat-seeking missile?"

Carl's gaze in my direction is followed by two of the committee's security detail, but I duck my head just in time.

Madame Chairman slams down her gavel so many times that I'm surprised it hasn't broken into splinters.

Like all good comedians, Carl waits until the audience has calmed down before continuing. "There were many things I had to do to prove myself to the terrorist's leaders, none of which I'm proud of. But the success of my mission speaks for itself—*I alone eliminated all twelve of the leaders in the international terrorist organization known as the Quorum.* My mission's success has been well-documented in a report that was submitted to President Chiffray within an hour of his being sworn into office, by the outgoing intelligence director, in fact. After reading it, the president handed a copy to Madame Chairman, along with his nomination letter."

Senator Kuley glares at his colleague. "Is this true?"

Vanna Ackerman gives him a slight nod.

"Why wasn't I, or the rest of the committee, privy to this so-called report?" Kuley roars at her.

She hits her gavel on its block. "If the great senator from Missouri will get ahold of himself, I'll very honestly and directly tell you that report's sensitivity is such that the redaction process is still in progress. You see, Lieutenant Stone's undercover status was compromised on numerous occasions by one of the community's most trusted contrac-tors, no less! It is a viper that our country has nursed to its bosom!" She is clasping her own 38DDs so hard that I'm surprised she can breathe at all.

Obviously, so is Jack, because he snickers until he is choking.

I'd think it were funny, too, if it hadn't dawned on me that Carl is about to get away with murder. Make that numerous murders, and attempted murders—not to mention a few conspiracies to commit treason, attempted terrorist acts, and seven years of negligence in regard to child support payments.

I'm about to say so, loud and proud, but Jack has slapped his hand over my mouth. In our relationship, keeping each other out of jail is the ultimate public display of affection, so I guess I can forgive him.

"Mr. Vice Chairman, I'm sorry that you and the others weren't aware of my endeavors prior to this hearing." Carl's loud sigh pointedly lays the blame at the feet of his predecessor. "And of course I welcome any further questions, after you do read it. That being said, let me assure you that my very first act as Director of Intelligence is to do a full audit of all contractors. As the Snowden and Grodin incidents have so glaringly exposed, many of those who are paid well to guard our greatest secrets are, in fact, our worst enemies."

I can't keep quiet anymore. "Takes one to know one!" I shout at the top of my lungs.

This time, Jack shoves me under the bench while the senate security guards ramp up their search for the heckler.

In that position, I can barely breathe, but I can still hear Carl as he declares, "Keeping this Committee fully and currently informed is not only the law, it is this position's solemn obligation. I say this not only as an intelligence-career professional, but as a citizen." He pauses, as if his thoughts are weighted down with the gravity of his convictions. "Madame Chairman, Mr. Vice Chairman, and other committee members, if confirmed, I pledge, not only to follow the law, but to go a step further and increase the trust between Congress and the DNI. In doing so, I will welcome any of your questions, and I invite you to hold me accountable, because our objective ought to be the same: to give the intelligence community all that it needs to succeed within the confines of our laws."

Senator Ackerman graces him with a smile. "Your superiors have no doubt about that. In fact, let me read this letter from the outgoing Director of Intelligence, who has given you his full endorsement—I'm so sorry, I mean *'had'* given. Unfortunately, General Benjamin Overton met with an unfortunate accident on his ranch this morning. The country, as a whole, mourns his loss deeply."

Game. Set. Match.

Following her reading of the dearly departed's letter, the rest of the committee—that is, everyone but C. Bright Kuley—applaud enthusiastically. Heck, why not? It's easier to let loose with a joyous huzzah in front of the cameras than to actually read the damn report, let alone poke holes in it.

They are joined by nearly all of the hearing's attendees.

Jack and I both need some fresh air. He pulls me off the floor, and out the back door, grumbling, "I can't wait to get my hands on that report."

I can, but I don't say that to him. If Carl's fantasy version has him wearing a humongous ten-gallon white hat, I can only imagine who will be portrayed as the bad guys.

He always did love me in black.

3

Strangers on a Train

"I still think it would be wonderful to have a man love you
so much he'd kill for you."

Patricia Hitchcock, as "Barbara Morton"

*THE TIGHT HALLS, INTIMATE CABINS, CURTAINED SLEEPING BERTHS.
The gentle clickity-clack and rhythmic thrusts of your iron horse's
steel wheels, as it makes its way down the tracks and into another
tunnel of love. All of this has you shouting, "Yes—yes—YES!" to
the question: "Can you still find romance on the rails?"*

Of course—just like in the movies!

*So that your journey is as satisfying as any you've seen on the
big screen, make sure your ticket to ride includes:*

1. *An overnight journey. Sure, you could do the down-
   and-dirty in the time it takes the Capitol Limited to go*

from Washington D.C.'s Union Station to Baltimore's Penn Station, but half the fun is getting there (the other half is the treasure chest of sex toys you've brought along) so sit back and enjoy the ride!

2. *A private cabin. Sorry, but two coach seats on the subway just won't cut it. No matter how much you loved* Risky Business, *let's face it: he's no Tom Cruise and you, madam, are no Rebecca De Mornay, so get a room—on a real train.*

3. *A little roleplaying. For example, the man in your life can be Cary Grant helping you—his Eva Marie Saint —up into the top bunk berth. Too tame? Then assign him the role of "Stern Conductor" and you can be "Naughty Stowaway."*

Better yet, switch roles. Even he'll concede that you look much better in that railway insignia cap and jacket when you're also wearing fishnet stockings and stiletto heels.

And if you get into your roles, you can make your own movie.

THE TEXT MESSAGE ON MY CELL PURRS, *LAST TRAIN FROM L'Enfant to Farragut West. Alone.* —CS (The One And Only)

No. Oh, no....

Somehow Carl has hacked my cell phone, and now he wants to see me.

Now that he's a shoo-in for full senate confirmation for the position of DI (apropos, considering he's such a DICK to begin with), I presume he wants to wipe the slate clean between us.

"Is that Ryan?" Jack comes over from the couch, curious as to why all the blood has drained from my face.

We are in our room at the L'Enfant Plaza hotel. It's now nine o'clock. We elected to have room service instead of going out to dinner, but neither of us has touched the food on our trays. The last seventy-two hours have been gruesome. Between the Yemen mission and today's follies, we're both dead on our feet.

"It's not Ryan, but…er, Jeff. He wants to know if he can stay up late and watch the end of the Broncos game. I think I'll let him. He's been very good about his homework."

"The Broncos, eh?" He smiles, but there is still curiosity in his eyes.

I click off my phone. "I'm jumping in the shower before Ryan gets here. I want to be bright-eyed and bushy-tailed for what he has to tell us about his dinner with Carl." I make myself smile. "Care to join me?"

He thinks for a moment but finally shakes his head. "You go on ahead. I haven't finished the Yemen report. It will be the cherry on the cake of Ryan's day."

"Maybe Ryan's meeting with Carl is a good sign for Acme. I mean, isn't it smarter to open all lines of communication, see if we can work out some sort of truce?" This might have sounded more believable if I hadn't said it in the same voice I use when I'm trying to get the kids to do something they consider a fate worse than death.

Jack is copping the same attitude, only in his case he

doesn't even bother to argue. Instead, he pointedly ignores my hopelessly inane remark and goes back to writing his report.

I head to the shower, closing the door behind me.

I don't want Jack to see me cry.

I've got to get all the fear out of my system.

I've got to get ready for battle.

AROUND TEN-THIRTY, WE HEAR A KNOCK ON OUR DOOR. JACK gets up and looks out the peephole to confirm it's Ryan, then he lets him in.

When it comes to showing emotions, Ryan rivals Mount Rushmore. Still, those of us who know him well have learned to read the smallest nuance in his stony demeanor. With a single blink, he telegraphs his disappointment. The tiny wrinkles around his eyes are hieroglyphics that spell danger. You can read the truth between his silences.

Jack and I watch as he belts back the scotch I offer him. When he finally speaks, it's with dead eyes. "Not only are we on the chopping block, we may find ourselves in jail, too. Acme will be the victim of Carl's witch hunt."

A trickle of dread runs down my spine. "What do you mean by that?"

Ryan shrugs. "If you haven't already guessed, the audit threat to quote-unquote, uncover attempts at treason is aimed at us."

Jack grimaces. "If anyone is treasonous, it's Carl. And we

can prove it—if we're ever given the chance. Will Chiffray at least listen to us?"

Ryan shakes his head. "He's still not returning my calls. And Carl was certainly not pleased with my attempts to contact POTUS. Tonight, he made it quite clear that, as far as the intelligence community is concerned, all roads to Chiffray go through him. In the meantime, I've got Arnie battening down the hatches around our intel infrastructure."

"Maybe a good night's sleep will bring a solution." Jack stifles a yawn. "What time does the Acme jet pull out for the west coast, boss?"

"Oh-nine-hundred." Ryan puts down his glass and heads for the door. "We can talk more about a defense strategy when we're airborne."

Jack walks him to the door, and locks it behind him.

We undress in silence.

I'm relieved he's too tired for sex. As for me, my body is energized—not for lovemaking, but for war.

I'll be packing heat and an assassin's blade.

I lay down beside Jack. Twenty minutes later, I hear his gentle snores.

Not a moment too soon. The L'Enfant Plaza Metro station is half a block away. Still, I'll have to hurry to keep the rendezvous. Quietly as I can, I rise and slip on my jeans, a sweater, my winter coat and my boots, as well as a G42, a switchblade, and a serrated knife.

A girl's got to accessorize, right?

Then I slip out of the room.

It's up to me to keep Acme in play, no matter what it takes.

THE LAST TRAIN LEAVES THE L'ENFANT PLAZA STATION AT exactly eleven-fifty-seven.

When I get to the station, it's empty. At least, that's what I'm supposed to believe. But the moment I get on the escalator that takes me down to the Blue Line platform, a man in a suit steps on behind me. Before I reach the platform, another man appears out of the shadows.

The train pulls up and screeches to a halt.

There is only one passenger: Carl.

Before boarding, I'm frisked by one of the men. He takes my cell and snaps it off. His pupils dilate when he comes across the gun hidden inside the pocket of my coat. As he pulls a switchblade from my boot, he mutters, "Jesus."

Carl chuckles. "Quite the little charmer, isn't she? Trust me, her cooking more than makes up for her paranoia."

I bat my eyes at the guy.

He missed the switchblade I've hidden up my coat sleeve. If I get a chance to use it, he better hope Carl doesn't live, because he'll end up in the cell next to mine, just for letting it slip by.

The men take their places in the cars on either side of this one. They stand sideways near the doors adjacent to it, so that they can watch us out of the corner of their eyes.

Carl doesn't get up.

So much for manners.

The train begins my trip to hell.

I don't offer my hand, or even a smile, but slip into the

seat across from him. "Did you really feel you needed back-up against little old me?"

"What can I say? My own battalion of storm troopers is one of the perks of my new position." He smiles. "You'll get to enjoy them, too, soon enough."

"Oh? How do you figure?"

"Ah, sweet wifey, you love to play hard to get, don't you?" He plops down in the seat next to me. "Let's stop the games. Time to kiss and make up."

He leans in to do just that.

I leap up. "Don't you dare."

He yanks me down into his lap. "Come on, admit it—you want it, too."

"Isn't that the defense of all rapists?" I nod toward the security detail behind him. "Aren't you worried about what your new cronies think of you?"

"Who, them? Nah. They're part of my well-trained monkey army. See no evil, hear no evil, speak no evil." He puts one hand on my breast—"I can do this"—while his other hand takes my hair in his fist and jerks my head back —"and this"—then he licks my neck, all the way up the side of my face—"and this."

A fist to the gut has him releasing my hair—"And I can do this"—I say, crushing my heel into his foot—"and this, and"— I flick the switchblade to his throat—"this."

When I look up, the security detail is standing in the doorway, their guns drawn.

Despite his pain, Carl coughs out a chuckle. Waving them off, he declares, "What can I say? She loves public displays of affection."

The men exchange concerned glances, but keep their guns steady—

Until the train jerks to a stop. "Smithsonian," pronounces a congenial automated female voice over the car's speakers.

The doors swing open, but the place is empty.

"If you're looking for a diversion or witnesses, forget it. My people took the precaution of clearing out every station between L'Enfant and West Farragut before we boarded. And yes, they will shoot you in the back if you run."

Okay then, I guess I should scratch "hasty retreat" off my must-do list.

"Donna, dearest, now that we have the foreplay out of the way, why don't we discuss a way to save Acme?"

Slowly I lower the switchblade and lean back. "I'm listening."

He smiles. "What I propose is simple. We end our interminable separation once and for all."

"You'll sign the divorce papers? Finally! Sure okay, I'll have Alan send them to your evil lair." *Free at last! Free at last!*

"You misunderstand me. The prodigal son—and daughter and other daughter, and let's not forget you, my sweet—are coming home—that is, here to DC, to live with me. I look forward to being clasped to the bosom of my family. Well, yours, anyway." He eyes me sideways. "Despite the fact they seem smaller than I remember."

Overhead, the automated female voice declares, "Federal Triangle Station."

Once again, the train slows to a stop.

Run, the little voice in my head tells me. I stare out at the station. Two exits, one with a set of stairs, another ascending via an escalator—

"Don't even think of it," Carl murmurs. He nods toward his monkey brigade.

I'd be shot before I made it past either of them.

The doors shut. The train takes off again.

I turn to him. "You're crazy! I'm not uprooting my children for you!"

"Oh, I'm not asking for me. You'd be doing it for Jack."

"Jack? Why would I leave him? He's been a better husband to me than you ever were."

"You feel that way about him, even without a ring on your finger, eh?" He clicks his tongue in mock dismay. "Granted, I can see why it works for him. Why buy the cow when you're already getting the milk?" His eyes slip down to my hips. "I'm not implying you're a heifer, but you are packing a few more pounds than the last time I saw you."

Keep your cool…Keep your cool…

I rise and walk toward the exit door. "This conversation is going nowhere."

"Donna, if you don't agree to my terms, everyone involved with Acme will be arrested and tried for treason. That includes your precious Jack, who'll wither away in a cell for life, if he doesn't get a lethal injection for the multiple murder charges I'll make sure he faces. One way or another, you'll get the '̓til death do you part' you seem to want so badly." A second later he's beside me again. "You're not above the law, either. I'll have you locked up on some trumped-up terrorism charge and make certain it's for life—unless you do as I say." He lifts my chin with his index finger so that I have nowhere to look except into his eyes. "In any event, our children will spend the rest of their lives with at least one of their biological parents, if not both. The choice is yours."

The choice is mine.

I can save Acme and Jack by spending the rest of my life with Carl, or I can risk losing my job, the man I love, and my children and end up in jail.

Tears suddenly fill my eyes.

He must see them because he's wearing his disgusting victory grin.

The next thing I know, he shoves me against the car's center pole and grinds his mouth into mine.

The train shudders to a stop.

He backs off. It's an involuntary reflex.

My involuntary reflex is to gag.

Instead, I succumb to a voluntary one and spit in his face.

Angrily, he wipes it off with the back of his hand. With the same hand, he slaps me—hard.

My head smacks into the pole, causing me to wince.

"I presume you've made your choice." He takes the kerchief from his breast pocket. Dabbing his face, he adds, "Sorry we have to do this the hard way." His slight nod brings his entire goon squad into our car. "Boys, you saw the little lady's switchblade, didn't you?"

Carl's goons nod ominously.

"Don't you feel the public would forgive you if she were accidentally shot trying to knife me, what with the cost of a jury trial and her time in the slammer?" He shakes his head.

"I've seen how much she eats. Believe me, we'd be saving a lot of hard-earned taxpayer dollars."

"We'd still have a lot of explaining to do to the press," says Goon Number One.

"Quick thinking, Dewey. You get an extra cookie with your milk at bedtime." Carl wrinkles his brow. "I guess she could commit hari-kari, right here in the car."

Oh.

Heck.

Then again, maybe not.

I'm trying hard to teach my kids to think positively, not negatively; to make lemonade from lemons; to be proactive as opposed to reactive.

It's time to lead by example.

"Metro Center," the auto-announcer cries out cheerily.

A second later, the doors open.

Dewey's reflection in the subway's window shows me he's close enough to slam in the gut with a back kick, no problem.

His gun flies out of his hand as he reels backward.

Hughey is aiming at me. (I really don't think that's his name. Still it's better than Goon Number 2.) But, he's not stupid enough to shoot in such narrow quarters, what with his boss standing between us.

This gives me time to roll for the gun—

Which I shoot because I have no qualms about killing Carl.

Hughey takes a slug in his wrist. When his gun falls to the floor, Carl scrambles for it. He grabs it and turns around to shoot—

But I'm gone.

The door slides shut behind me.

Carl runs to it and slams it hard, but it won't open.

I smile pretty. I wave *Bye-bye.*

A second later, the train is roaring down the track.

I flop onto the floor, gasping for breath.

When I can breathe again, I run up the escalator, two steps at a time.

JACK IS SLEEPING SOUNDLY. HE DOESN'T STIR AS I UNDRESS, NOT even as I get into bed beside him.

As I spoon him from behind, he mutters, "Your feet are ice cold."

"Maybe I need something to warm them up."

He flips around so that we're nose to nose. "I could rub them."

"That sounds nasty."

"I meant with my feet, silly woman."

"Rub something else. Preferably not with your feet."

He doesn't need a written invitation.

His hand is slow, and gentle. So are his lips, upon mine.

Ah, yes, he's warmed me up. All my senses are on fire.

When he enters me, I am frenetic. I am alive.

I am frightened.

I beg him to stop, but it's too late: I'm already outside the stratosphere of physical control and moving at warp speed toward the planet Euphoria.

There I hover, inert and joyous—

Until the inevitable: I crash, back here on Earth.

I have yet to recover when he whispers in my ear, "Don't worry, Donna. Carl can't hurt us."

I sigh.

I wish I could believe that.

———————————————————

4

Sunset Boulevard

———————————————————

"Sometimes it's interesting to see just how *bad* bad writing can be. This promised to go the limit."

William Holden, as ˮJoe Gillisˮ

EVERYONE'S LIFE IS THE STUFF MOVIES ARE MADE FROM.

Admit it, if Hollywood came a-knockin' on your front door with a contract to turn your life into a movie or a reality show, you'd be sooooo there.

Maybe it's time for a reality check as to what they'll do with the life you hold nearest and dearest — your own:

- *Reality Check #1: Your life story isn't worth a plug nickel. If you're banking on more, don't. The producer's offer will be piddly, because he thinks (and he's right) that your ego will win out over your need for a few more bucks in your bank account. Not only that, whatever option money you agree to will come in after certain production hurdles are crossed (Translation: finding backers, a.k.a., the funding!) and your talent agent and entertainment lawyers slice off their own flesh-eating fees.*

Hey, you'll be lucky if the producer doesn't hit you up to help fund the flick in exchange for an "executive producer" credit.

- *Reality Check #2: Don't expect the script to truly reflect your experiences in any way, shape or form. There is a reason movies based on real people or incidents all start off with the disclaimer, "Inspired by…" which is even more of a tip-off than "Based on…"*

Bottom line: Your story may have taken place in Peoria, but it won't play well there. That said, expect a few embellishments, and perhaps a whopper or two.

- *Reality Check #3: You, madam, are no Erin Brockovich —so don't expect Julia Roberts to play you in the movie. That also goes for Charlize Theron, Jennifer Lawrence, and Scarlett Johansson.*

(Okay, maybe Meryl Streep, but only because she can play anyone. Lucky you!)

∼

"ONE DOUBLE ESPRESSO, EXTRA SLOW DRIP, FOR DUDE Lebowski!" the Starbucks Barista shouts over the murmurs of patrons.

"Wait…the Dude is *here*?" a customer asks loudly.

All heads turn in order to scrutinize everyone within sight, cell phones poised to take a picture of anyone even resembling Jeff Bridges.

Arnie starts over to the counter, but I grab his arm and pull him back. "Way to go, genius! We're supposed to be incognito, remember? If you go over there, everyone in the place will stare right at us."

Arnie shrugs sheepishly. "When the cashier asked what name to put on the cup, Lebowski was the first one that came to mind."

Ryan buries his head in his hands. I don't blame him. Life keeps dealing him one blow after another.

The new Director of Intelligence has done exactly as he promised the committee: he's cleaning house of contractors he deems traitorous. No doubt, heads will roll, subpoenas will fly, and culprits will feel the long arm of the law—as defined by Carl Stone.

And thanks to my refusal to leave Jack, guess who's first on his hit list?

Since last week, Acme's offices have been shuttered by the Department of Justice. All files and computers have been seized, along with its bank accounts.

And all of Acme's operatives have scattered to the wind—

Except for the ones on my mission team: Jack, Arnie, Abu, Emma, Dominic and, of course, me.

Jack still doesn't know about Carl's request. I plan on keeping it this way. He loves me and the children, but I have no doubt he'd make the sacrifice that would keep the nation secure from Carl and his devious schemes.

The first consequence of my declaration of war with my soon-to-be ex is that every move we make is being watched. It's an exhausting game of cat-and-mouse. Should they find us congregating in any fashion, they'll assume the worst—which, in this case, is also the truth:

With or without the sanction of our own government, we're sworn to take down the Quorum.

And since Carl still runs it, we have to take him down, too.

To shake the agents who are tailing us, Jack and I have established a pattern that is typical of any Hilldale couple. In the morning, we head off in different directions as we carpool our children to school. Afterwards, we run our separate errands. Mine take me to the grocery store, the mall, perhaps the hair salon or nail studio. Jack usually ends up at Home Depot, the bank, or the country club for a game of golf.

Throughout the day, like other loving couples, we send each other lovey-dovey emails or texts intercutting mundane requests with terms of endearments. For example, Jack will ask me, his "Poochie-Smoochie," to pick up his favorite suit from the dry-cleaners, whereas I'll remind Jack, a.k.a., "Studmuffin," to buy dog food.

In truth, these loving reminders use coded phrases relaying the who-what-where-when and how of our next rendezvous with the rest of our Acme team: Ryan, Dominic, Abu, Arnie and Emma.

By lunchtime, we're home again. Usually, we spend our afternoons exchanging mundane gossip, checking our email—

And making love.

Loud, hot, steamy sex.

At least, that's what it sounds like to those listening in.

During these supposed sessions of afternoon delight, the curtains are drawn in the bedroom. Every now and then a shadow in the window can be mistaken for a couple in the throes of passion. In truth, it is a reflection from a light box, timed to appear during a dialogue consisting of naughty talk laced with a litany of sensual moans.

We certainly know how to put on a show.

While our audience is enthralled, we walk out the back door, leap over the fence, grab an unregistered car, and head to the agreed-upon assignation.

Today's missive, which I received from my manicurist during a pedicure, sent us to this Starbuck's, in Manhattan Beach. We've been taking our cue from start-ups and the self-employed and are making any space offering free WiFi our office away from home.

Before Arnie can blow the lid on our seemingly innocent gathering, I grab his arm. "Don't go," I warn him. "Instead, order the same thing under a different name—something innocuous, like 'John Brown.'" My own fake moniker for my caramel macchiato is as plain Jane as can be—Susan Smith.

As he nods, the barista calls out, "Dominic Fleming, your martini, shaken with a twist, is ready!"

Ryan slams his hand on the coffee table in front of us. "What part of 'covert' do you people not understand?"

Jack looks up from the newspaper he's reading. "Wait… they serve martinis here, too?"

"Usually after four, but they bend the rules for those who merit it." Dominic waves grandly at the barista. "Thank you, my good man. Kindly send someone over with it."

Jack throws the paper on the coffee table. "This joint is self-serve. What makes you think the kid is going to run over with your drinkie-poo?"

"Ah, here it is now." Dominic graces the girl who delivers it with a smile.

She preens—and then writes her telephone number on a napkin before sauntering off.

"That's it," Ryan growls. "Next time, we meet in a cemetery."

"Great idea, boss," Emma exclaims cheerfully. "Maybe we can find an empty mausoleum."

I shudder. "Thanks, but no thanks. I've had my fill of tombs."

"No problem there—at least, not in the near future. In fact, all travel to exotic locales will be a thing of the past if Acme doesn't replace the revenue that just flew out the door with Carl's appointment." It's that thought, not the café's Gold Coast blend, that has Ryan grimacing as he sips his coffee. "Not only are the Feds climbing up our asses with proctoscopes, but every one of our clients and assets—both domestically and internationally—have been interrogated about us."

"Doesn't anyone find it odd that the previous Director of

Intelligence died the day after he retired to his Montana ranch?" asks Emma.

"Of course they do," Jack assures her. "Not to mention that the cause of death—being trampled by a herd of Black Angus steers that were his pride and joy—isn't exactly normal."

"All the more reason to erase any evidence that may land us in jail, if it can't be validated as a sanctioned operation. I've no doubt Arnie scrubbed our hard drives to a fare-thee-well," Ryan muses out loud. "But ask yourself: why are we being tailed? Carl is on a fishing expedition, and Acme is his Moby Dick."

"Ryan's right," Dominic says, as he plucks the olive from the toothpick in his drink. "In fact, things may be worse than we know. My contact in Morocco tells me that there's a reward being offered to anyone with proof that Acme has, quote, performed deeds that can be considered detrimental to the security of the country, unquote."

"That's ridiculous," Abu sputters. "Every one of Acme's missions were sanctioned—if not by the US intelligence community, then by POTUS himself."

"I've set up a meeting with POTUS, to personally hand over validated evidence of all Acme mission orders. But until he clears us of all charges, we've each got a target over our heads. Needless to say, no foreign governments will hire us, either." Ryan winces. "In the meantime, we all have bills to pay—which brings me to one job that has fallen into our laps. It's not our usual mission. Hell, it's not a mission at all."

Jack leans forward. "You mean, a corporate security or espionage gig?"

"Ha, I wish! Sadly, our new reputation precedes us into Fortune 500 boardrooms as well." Ryan attempts a smile, but it's as tepid as the coffee in his cup. "We've been asked to consult on a movie—an espionage thriller. The producer is Addison Montague. Apparently, the film will star Leo DiCaprio and Amy Adams. Martin Scorsese is onboard to direct. As you can imagine, with that A Team, they want to be as authentic as possible."

"What a relief," sniffs Dominic. "None of that *Bourne* or *Mission Impossible* silliness."

Ryan nods. "That's exactly how Montague put it. He's looking for two consultants with field experience to vet the script, as well as a tech equipment advisor on the set during production."

Arnie practically hits the ceiling with his fist pump. "I am so in!"

Ryan doesn't flinch. "I had no doubt about it. As for those of you with field experience, they'll want to meet with you later today—two o'clock, at Montague's offices, on Sunset. Who's in? Let's see a show of hands."

Mine goes up, as does Dominic's.

Ryan glances over at Jack. "You don't want to be considered?"

Jack shrugs. "I don't audition."

Dominic gives his shoulder a sympathetic pat. "Can't say I blame you, old boy. No need to have one's nose rubbed ignominiously against the obvious."

Jack frowns. "And what do you mean by that?"

Condescension roils in Dominic's chuckle. "Why even bother, when I'm so obviously better suited for the position?" A quick glance at his Omega has him rising gracefully out of his wingback. "Ah! I'll just have time for a quick facial before the meeting." He looks down at me. "Shall I pick you up before heading over, dear? Heaven knows what they'll think of you if you drive up in your mommy mobile. Not quite the roadster they'd envision for a femme fatale."

He's got a point. Still, the stony look on Jack's face is reason enough to pass, even if it means heading over on Mary's bicycle.

"Not to worry," I murmur. "I'll meet you there." I turn to Abu. "You've got field experience. Why don't you put yourself up for it, too?"

Abu snorts. "What, are you kidding? Nah, I've got a better idea of how I can wait out this temporary economic downturn: a cupcake shop. You know, one of those gourmet joints, with a party room and all. And Dominic has given me a great idea—to get a liquor license while I'm at it." He smiles. "I've got the perfect location picked out. Send over some of your wonderful recipes, and I'll cut you in for five percent."

"Works for me." We shake on it. Then I whisper, "How are you going to break the news to Ryan?"

"Don't worry about that. He'll see the benefit. At the very least, we'll have a place to meet without worrying about who's listening in."

True, that.

And a place to drink, too. If Dominic or I blow this

opportunity to keep Acme's doors open, we'll all be looking for a place to drown our sorrows.

"You're what they call a 'honeypot,' right? How many men have you killed?"

This is how Addison Montague introduces himself after he's kept me—under the alias of "Jane Smith"—cooling my heels in his reception area for the past hour while he manned the phone, yelling at (a) the agent of an aging action star who drinks too much on location for a movie currently in production, (b) the lawyer of a rising starlet-slash-former-porn-star who refuses to do a nude scene, although it's in her contract, and (c) his travel agent, who wants to know what to do since both his wife and his mistress want to plan getaways with him for the coming weekend.

I should have walked out thirty minutes ago, but I'm here to win the job—unlike Dominic, who is nowhere to be seen. That must be some facial he's getting.

The past hour and a half has given me plenty of time to stare at the posters from Addison's box office successes. More importantly, I've also had a few minutes to access his INTERPOL dossier. What I've read is both impressive and depressing. Despite having won his fair share of Oscars, Cannes Film Festival Palme d'Ors, and Sundance Film Festival Grand Jury prizes, it's his casting couch prowess that has catapulted him to the pinnacle of Hollywood's star-studded firmament.

After taking a moment to at least pretend to consider his

question about my own street cred, I look up from the script in my hand, which has kept me less than enthralled. "My kill rate is in the mid-double digits."

Addison's unibrow rises so high I'm afraid it'll knock that ridiculous toupee off his head. He's practically salivating as he asks, "Tell the truth—do you get off on it?"

I hope the spittle on the side of his mouth isn't an indication of his own bedside manner—not that I plan on finding out personally. I shrug. "It's a gig, like any other. You make movies, I save the world." I hold up the screenplay, *Lethal*. "But, to be honest, I don't think you can save this project—at least, not the way it's now written."

Addison takes that as an open invitation to sidle up next to me. "Oh yeah? What's wrong with it?" He leans in so close that now I'm using the script as a shield.

If he keeps this up, he'll be the next notch on my belt.

"If you must know, it's got a great high concept, but it's filled with all the typical thriller clichés that will have the critics calling it crap." Both Addison and I turn to see Jack, leaning against the door.

"Who the hell are you?" Addison asks.

"John Smith." Jack smiles. "And her husband. Not that it matters. The way this is written, you'll have a hell of a time selling it to your usual money men."

Addison may be talking to Jack, but he only has eyes for me. "How do you figure?"

I'm about to give him my take on it, but before I can open my mouth, Jack says, "Your hero should have balls of steel. Instead he's got a wrist so limp, it's a wonder he can hold up his martini glass. What's worse, you've got a buffoon for a villain, and one of those heroines who's homely until she takes off her glasses and loosens her fun bun—then, all of a sudden, she's a fox? Give me a break."

"Anything else?" Addison is now so close that I can smell what he had for lunch: I'm guessing rack of lamb at the Ivy.

"Sure," Jack retorts. "The gadgets mentioned in this toilet paper of a script are so antiquated that this could have been written during the first Gulf War. Oh, and by the way, the farthest a sniper bullet has killed was just over twenty-seven hundred yards, so your writer is way off the mark there, too."

"Twenty-three or twenty-four hundred, however, is more realistic," I chime in. "My farthest hit was twenty-two-fifty."

Jack shakes his head. "Honey, if you're thinking of the Rio mission, it was eighteen-hundred, tops."

"Sweetheart, you're wrong," I say through a flash of smiling gritted teeth. "I should know because *I was the one doing the shooting—remember?*"

Jack sighs loudly. "Now, now, cupcake, give me some credit. I was there, too—and standing right next to the target."

"'Standing?' Ha! You were *dancing* with that over-inflated hussy—"

"A basic two-step. No twerking"—Jack winks knowingly at Addison—"but she was a grinder."

The producer chuckles cautiously. I think he's figured out he's in over his head with us.

"Next time, *darling,* instead of whispering sweet nothings in her ear, figure out a way to get *out* of my crosshairs." I pucker into a pout. "Things could have been a bit messy if you'd embraced her right when I pulled the trigger."

Addison's eyes grow big. "You shot her—while he was holding her?"

"It's okay. The woman was already dead." Jack looks over at Addison and pantomimes a knife slicing a neck. "What Donna neglected to mention was that she was aiming for the guy next to us."

"Yeah, alright, I was off by six inches! So sue me." I flutter my lashes at Addison. "The second shot's always the charm."

Addison edges away from me—but when he realizes he's now standing next to Jack, he slides back toward me.

The lesser of two evils, I guess.

The three of us stand there for a long minute. Finally Addison nods. "Well, Mr. and Mrs. Smith, when can you start?"

"What exactly does the job entail?" I ask.

"You'll take a second, more detailed, look at the script. If it's as bad as you say, it'll need a re-write. But it's got to be a fast one. Otherwise we'll lose our stars and our director. You'll have to hole up with the screenwriter. I'll reserve a couple of suites at the Sunset Tower. I'm offering two thousand a day, starting tomorrow. You'll be paid when he turns in the script, which should be within a week or so.'

Jack smiles. "Two thousand a day—apiece, right?"

"Sure. Two"—Addison's gaze shifts in my direction —"apiece."

I don't like the way he says that.

I can tell Jack doesn't either, because his grin fades away.

"Yeah, okay. Send the paperwork to my email. We don't get paid on the back end. Instead we start the moment the first check clears the bank." He holds out his hand to Addison.

The producer laughs. "Quaint," he says, as he shakes it.

When I do the same, he pulls me in close.

Wrong move. I twist his arm behind his back and drive his face into the wall.

"How did you know I like it rough?" he gasps. "Honey, if this is any indication of what you're like in the sack, there's an extra five grand in it for you, any night you're free."

All it would take to put this slime bucket out of his misery is a quick twist of his neck. But I back off.

Jack knows it, too, which is why he jerks Addison's arm even harder, to the point the guy is whimpering. "Donna is not one of your starlets," he mutters into Addison's ear. "Deal's off."

"Hey, it was an honest mistake!" Addison yells after us, as Jack pulls me out the door with him. "Okay, I'll make it three...three and a half—but that's my final offer!"

"So, it's come to this?" I rant over the honk of six lanes of Sunset Boulevard traffic, as we walk through the studio lot to our cars. "We're down to proofing scripts for lascivious Hollywood producers?"

"This is Hollywood." Jack pulls open my car door for me. "Here, dignity is just another four-letter word."

Suddenly I'm hyperventilating. "We just turned down thirty-five hundred a day. Ryan isn't going to be too pleased."

"Not to worry. We'll keep it our little secret from the boss man, until you choose to do otherwise," Jack says, in a perfect imitation of Dominic, speaking the Queen's English.

His damn accent is so good that I quit crying and start laughing. "Speaking of Dominic, why wasn't he here?"

"He's much too proud to take a meeting with Addison."

"Are you kidding me? He was wetting his pants to apply for this gig."

"Not after his face broke out."

"But…how could that be? It's always as smooth as an infant's ass."

"Apparently, the mush his facialist slathered on him contained poison oak spores. Go figure." He ducks his head so that I can't see his grin.

"Gee, that certainly was convenient—for you."

"Yeah, I thought so, too. But now, I guess Dominic will get the job after all."

"I don't think so. Not after your 'limp-wristed' martini remark."

"Then it'll go to one of the many other black-op groups. We'll just have to come up with some other scheme to pay the bills."

He kisses me, then heads toward his own car.

I guess he can always teach dance lessons. And I've got my cupcake recipes…

Oh, who the hell am I kidding? We're guns for hire.

Or for revenge.

5

The Fugitive

"What I want from each and every one of you is a hard-target search of every gas station, residence, warehouse, farmhouse, henhouse, outhouse and doghouse in that area…Go get him."

Tommy Lee Jones, as "Deputy Marshall Samuel Gerard"

IN CONTRADICTION TO THE LEGENDARY ACTRESS GRETA GARBO, not every star wants to be alone.

At least, that's what you tell yourself as you stalk your celebrity du jour, isn't it?

You fantasize some cute meet, perhaps at his favorite dry cleaners, or at his gym. But when you stake out both of these places day after day in the hope of running into him, you're shooed away by your beloved's bodyguards. Not fair!

You get a job at his favorite restaurant under the assumption that eventually he'll notice how you honor his every whim—or better yet, that you'll be what he requests for dessert. But when you poison his steady girlfriend's Stevia, once again, fingers point in your direction. Not fair!

You've outdone yourself when you get hired as his housekeeper, but your very first day at work is ruined when his trusty watchdog recognizes your scent as his master's stalker, and he has you running out the gate—

And into the arms of the man you were meant to share your life with.

No, he's not a star. He's just a sweet guy who'll love you for being yourself.

The next time you see your celebrity du jour—in some tabloid magazine—you wonder what you ever saw in him in the first place—

And thank your lucky stars you shook that poisoned Stevia rap before you met your Mr. Right.

My beautiful home sits dead center on Hilldale's last street of monster mansions, where the backyards' velvety lawns end beside an eight-foot ivy-covered brick wall flanking the farthest side of our gated community. The community's park is several streets over, at the end of Hill-dale's main boulevard, so for the most part we're off the parade path of tricycles, scooters, skaters, running children, and mothers pushing strollers heading to the playground.

With the line of work we're in, I don't mind living on the quietest street in town.

To keep my mind off Acme's travails, I've kept myself busy all morning with mundane housework. The kitchen is spotless. Laundry has been washed, dried, separated, and now folded, at the foot of my children's beds. I've just started the task of putting Trisha's toys back on the shelf beneath her window when I notice that a woman with a fairly large perambulator has stopped in front of our house. She bends over the stroller as if tucking a blanket around the baby inside of it.

There is no baby. Instead, she's taking a picture of our house. From where I stand, the camera's lens, which is tucked into the hood of the stroller, is reflecting a ray of sunlight.

I presume the words she murmurs into the carriage aren't sweet endearments for her invisible child, but some sort of message, which can be heard in the ear buds of her fellow operatives, who are no doubt close by.

I step back from the window. After waiting for my heart to calm down, I take off toward the attic stairs, where so much more is revealed from the vantage point of one of the front gable windows. Down the block, a Southern California Edison utility van sits next to the curb. Its license plate proves it's not owned by the company. The couple sitting in the Cramers' gazebo wears dark glasses, so I can't see which way their eyes are looking. From the angle of their heads—straight ahead—it's obvious they aren't reading the open books in their hands. The other telltale sign is that they don't even faintly resemble the Cramers.

But it's the caravan of black SUVs pulling up to Hilldale's gated entrance that has me running downstairs, where Jack sits with his computer, sifting through the massive Quorum intelligence he's collected over the years.

"Plan B," I shout as I grab a couple of the cloth grocery bags by the front door and start stuffing them with the things most important to me: those things in my living room curio cabinet, which include my personal journals, my children's very first stuffed animals, and the box holding the jewelry my mother left me.

Those two words tell him all he needs to know: *we're under attack.*

He stares at me. "I take it this is not a drill."

"Does this look like a drill to you?" I run past him into the kitchen, and open the back door. My high-pierced whistle sends our dogs, Lassie and Rin Tin Tin, scrambling into the house.

The sound of my snapping fingers sends them downstairs, into the basement and ready to await my next command.

If only Jack were half as obedient. I whistle at him, too, but he waves me off with one hand while he taps out a text on his cell.

If he blows our escape, he won't get any treats from me for a very long time.

I leap over the coffee table, toward the fireplace, where a portrait of my children hangs over the mantle, and shove it aside so that I can get to the switch code that sets off our escape plan.

Jack lifts himself off the couch, and stretches, as if he's got all the time in the world. "You know, once you arm the code, there's no turning back."

Yes, his warning gives me reason to pause. When I moved into the house with Carl, it was a very important milestone in our lives. I think of all the memories this home holds for me and my children—and Jack, too.

I remember the first time we made love here.

With the tap of a few buttons, our lives will never be the same.

Nothing in life is permanent. We adapt to survive.

And we never surrender.

We both know it. This resolve is reflected in his eyes.

My actions are validated by what we can now see on the screen of his cell: a line of tiny dots moving toward our house and congregating on the street just beyond the sidewalk.

I punch in the code, then run down the basement stairs.

Jack is at my heels with the bags of our most precious possessions slung over his shoulder.

Up against the brick wall on the far side of the basement is a built-in floor-to-ceiling storage unit that holds our children's board games, Lego bins and sports paraphernalia. The wall has already slid to one side, exposing a secret passageway for an underground tunnel. As soon as we pass through the entry's fireproof steel door, we'll push buttons on another code pad. The door will close and lock behind us, and the brick wall will cover it once again.

The dogs are already inside the tunnel. They run ahead, curious to see where it leads. When they get to the end, they won't recognize their whereabouts: the basement of a squalid little cottage—a safe house a half-mile beyond Hilldale's stately walls.

Above us now, several blocks away, natural gas, leaking from an unlit hot water heater has already set off a series of explosions in my house, turning it into a roaring inferno that no SWAT member will dare enter, let alone the Hilldale Fire Department.

They will have to wait until things cool down to discover the cause of the explosion, and the fact that no one was killed or injured.

By then, the family Stone will be long gone.

But first things first: pick up the kids from school.

The garage of the safe house holds two SUVs. Jack tosses me the keys to one as he jumps into the other. But before he has time to put the key into the ignition, his cell beeps with a text message. He reads it and sighs. "Ryan's attempt to clear Acme of Carl's bogus charges has failed." Jack shakes his head in disbelief. "The reason for the SWAT team is that we're being sought for the murder of Jonah Breck. Carl has had the webcam footage from Misfit Quay doctored to show that you're the one who killed Breck. Lee Chiffray is livid. Apparently Carl had the audacity to show it to him while Babette was in the room."

"I can only imagine her reaction." As much as Babette hated her deceased first husband, even she'd be horrified to think I killed him.

After all, our daughters do play together.

"At the same time," Jack continues, "the footage also shows what looks like me putting a bullet into the woman Breck was raping—Antoinette." The poor girl was the nanny of his daughter, Janie, whom he'd brought to his private island as a sex slave.

"But—Carl killed both of them!"

"Until we can prove it, we're considered murderers. Listen, you grab Trisha and Mary. I'll pick up Jeff. We'll rendezvous at Hilldale Mall, in front of the Cineplex. We can hide out in the movies until we can figure out where we go from here." He hesitates. "You know, Donna, it might mean leaving the country."

"I…I know that." I can barely think, I'm so upset. "But I'm not going without the children! I can't leave them here with Carl!"

"That will never happen. At least, not while either of us is alive."

The task at hand is to stay that way, despite what Carl has in store for us.

MY FIRST STOP IS HILLDALE ELEMENTARY FOR MY YOUNGEST daughter, Trisha. She loves her school, but movies are her passion. She'll look forward to playing hooky.

She may have to get used to it, until I research which countries don't have extradition clauses with the United States.

I turn my head, pretending to peruse the trophy case, just as two men in black suits and dark glasses march into the lobby. Identifying themselves to the receptionist as NSA agents, they then tersely request to speak to the principal, Miss Darling.

At first, the receptionist is flustered. But she quickly buzzes her boss.

Because the back of the trophy case is mirrored, I'm able to witness Miss Darling's reaction to the news that Jack and I are persons-of-interest, and that should either of us come for Trisha, she should call them immediately. In fact, they'll be in the parking lot, to see if they can intercept me prior to pick-up.

Miss Darling's faint nod assures them that she understands the severity of their mission. But as she catches my eye in the mirror, she mouths, *go*.

I will forever be in her debt.

In fact, this has convinced me to volunteer as the chairwoman for the school's live auction. I vow that it will be the most successful fundraiser in the history of the school. Of course, with what she's just been told by the NSA, I wouldn't blame her if she makes me swear on a stack of Bibles that none of the auction money raised was stolen from the US Treasury.

Miss Darling invites them into her office while she fills out a parking lot permit for them. "I'd hate for one of our volunteer parking monitors to have you towed. The parents here can be pretty aggressive. You know how it is when a little power goes to one's head."

With Carl in charge, I guess they've already found out. Now, I have, too.

After she shuts her office door, I move quickly toward Trisha's classroom. Her teacher, Miss McGonagall, sees me, and motions for Trisha, who runs to me.

I can't go out the front entrance because the NSA agents are, once again, in the front lobby. While a couple of fourth graders corner the NSA agents to ask if their guns have real bullets, Trisha and I slip out a side door.

No need to give them a reason to prove it.

I pray I don't have the same reception waiting for me at Hilldale High School. Mary already considers her family just borderline presentable. A perp walk in front of her peers will be just the sort of embarrassment that will have her begging off school for the rest of her life.

She may just get her wish.

"I've never been so embarrassed in my whole life! Mom, why did you have the principal pull me out of my chemistry class—during the middle of a test, no less?" Mary jumps into the SUV, slamming the door behind her. She stares at Trisha, then turns to me. "What's Trisha doing here?"

"We're playing hooky!" her little sister declares.

Before I turn around to face her, I lift my lips into an innocent smile. "I thought you wouldn't mind. Kids your age are under too much pressure." I hate lying to her, but better that than having her learn that her parents are now on the lam.

"I'm glad you think so. I'll give you a list of all my test days. Of course, then they'll hold me back and I'll never get into college."

"See? You just proved my point. You worry too much! And besides, your father has a new project that will take us on the road—for quite some time, the way it looks now. He wants us to join him, which will give us the chance for some real family adventures—starting today, in fact."

Mary's eyes narrow. "In the middle of a school year?"

"Sure, why not? I'll clear it with your principals. You can turn in your homework via email."

"I don't know. I mean…well, I guess it makes sense—since we didn't have much of a vacation last summer."

She's got a point there. We may have been on a resort called Fantasy Island, but that tropical paradise was anything but fun and games. Jack and I were almost killed—he, by pygmies, and me, by a cannibal serial killer. Did I mention I was almost sold into slavery? Some vacation. No five-star Expedia review there.

Then we came home to a few intense weeks of guarding presidential candidates. Despite keeping them alive, we couldn't keep their campaigns from imploding in one scandal after another. As it turns out, the top contender—my old high school frenemy, Catherine Martin—didn't win after all. It may have had something to do with the hit she put out on her own husband. Go figure.

She is now in prison. Mary stays in touch with her teenage son, Evan, who is finishing his junior year back in DC. Having been there when his life was destroyed by the loss of both his parents has made Mary quite introspective these days.

All the more reason she can't lose Jack or me right now.

So I put on my best Mary Poppins happy face. "First stop, the mall," I say brightly. "We're meeting the boys there, to take in a family movie."

Here's hoping there's not a SWAT team waiting for us when we get there.

WE PULL UP TO THE RENDEZVOUS SPOT—IN FRONT OF THE Hilldale Mall Cineplex to discover that the boys are already there.

By boys, I mean Jack and Jeff—and surprise, surprise, Jeff's two besties, Cheever Bing and Morton Smith.

Seeing them, I don't know who groans the loudest— Mary, Trisha, or me.

"I thought you said this was going to be a family outing," Mary grumbles.

"I'm just as surprised to see the Two Stooges as you are." I slip Trisha out of her seat belt and booster seat. "Take your sister inside to the movie snack bar, while I see why we're being made to suffer."

Slapping Cheever on the back of the head, Morton shouts, "Last one in is a rotten egg."

Cheever grabs Morton in a headlock and smacks him with a noogie. "What are you talking about? The only one who smells as if he crapped in his pants is you!"

Jack is quite adept at reading the look on my face. "Look, before you blame me for this, let's just say that it was easier to dodge the NSA agents by having all three boys with me. The last place they were staking out was the carpool lane. Besides, had I left Cheever and Morton at the school without a ride, we'd have more to worry about from mommy dearest, Penelope Bing, than any NSA agents."

Aw, heck, I forgot it was our afternoon to carpool. "Okay, so now what do we do with them? If we cross the border, it's kidnapping!"

"After the movie, we'll toss them out of the car in front of their homes. In the meantime, they'll keep the others occupied while we figure out what's happening." He pulls out his cell. "I'll try to reach Ryan while you go in there and try to keep the peace."

If only the roles were reversed—for the kids' sake, not mine. If Cheever and Morton start their shenanigans during the film, there won't be any "happily ever after" ending.

THE SNACK BAR LINE IS SNAKING THROUGH THE LOBBY. THE hold-up is Cheever. I can barely see his head over the humongous bag of popcorn in his arms.

"Mommy, is Cheever going to share with us?" Trisha asks.

Cheever finds this idea so ludicrous that he doubles over in laughter. This causes him to tilt his Giganta-Gulp drink cup. The seven candy bars slip out of his hands, too. I catch them before he drops everything. The last thing I need is to have him begin his trip to bountiful all over again.

"This is enough food for a small third-world country," I admonish him.

"That's because Mr. Stone says he's treating." He nods towards the register. "So, pay the cashier, okay?"

"That would mean taking out a small loan," I grumble, but I do as I'm told.

I'm about to follow Trisha into the theater showing the latest gem from Pixar when I notice the boys heading toward the latest Quentin Tarantino movie. I grab Jeff by the collar. "No, no, no, no! You and your friends are staying with us."

Jeff looks horrified. "Mom, we're not seeing some baby movie!"

Morton shakes his head adamantly. "What if someone sees us go in there?"

I can't tell him this, but that's the whole point—that no one finds us.

"To hell with that," Cheever chimes in. "We'll be the laughingstock of the whole middle school!"

"Pixar films are witty, and appropriate for any age," I argue. "The animation is always cutting edge."

My argument is falling on deaf ears. From Mary's wince, I can tell she agrees with the Two Stooges.

I'm adamant about one thing. "We're sticking together. There are seventeen films here, so let's take a vote."

The children scan the marquees that run down the long corridor in front of us.

"I vote for *She's So Hot*," Cheever says.

Trisha stares at the movie's poster, which features a big-breasted blonde being ogled by three men. Tiny horns on her head and the smoke billowing around her barely-there red negligee are supposed to give viewers the impression that the actress is a she-devil. "Mommy, why are her clothes too small?" she asks.

Jeff can't peel his eyes away from the poster, either. "Heck yeah, I second that motion."

"I third it," Morton chimes in.

Cheever shoves him. "You can't 'third' something, you moron."

I stand in front of the poster, but no amount of arm-waving will break the spell it has on my son. "Nope! Not an option. Any movie we choose together must be PG-rated, and no higher."

Jack sprints over to us. "This is the one we're seeing? Great! Super! Let's get in there before we miss all those great coming attractions."

The boys hi-five each other as they scurry in.

I'm just about to tell Jack that I think he's lost his mind when he whispers into my ear, "They're here!"

He then puts his arm around my waist, and practically shoves me into the theater with him.

As Trisha and Mary follow us into the dark theater, I hear Trisha whisper, "The devil woman looks scary."

"What's even more frightening is the way these kinds of movies objectify women," Mary hisses back. "They're either virgins, or she-devils."

"What's a virgin?" Trisha asks.

I'm relieved the music score blares so loudly that it's futile for Mary to answer her. I look back and catch Mary's eye. She knows what I'm thinking: that this is a question I'd prefer to field myself.

Certainly not this year.

Hopefully, I can stay out of jail long enough to be there when the time is right.

～

SMACK DAB IN THE MIDDLE OF THE THEATER, TRISHA SITS IN Mary's lap. She clasps both hands over her eyes when she thinks the action on the screen is too silly to watch—in other words, every other scene.

Smart girl. Wish I could do the same, but I've got my eye on the men in black, walking up and down the aisle as they search for America's Most Wanted couple.

Willow Higginbotham is a staple in numerous movies with a similar tone: light, frothy comedies filled with tongue-in-cheek double-entendres and plenty of opportunities to show off her scantily-clothed, well-toned physique. And yet, in the entertainment magazines that fill the racks next to the grocery store check-out land, the actress openly bemoans the fact that she's being typecast as a sex symbol. "I am *sooooo* ready for meatier roles—you know, something that will show my full range."

From what I can see on these magazine covers, her range goes from A to B—that is to say, ass to breasts.

Apparently, Jeff and his buddies feel the same way. The boys sit front and center, their eyes glued to the screen in order to catch every slapstick antic—and there are plenty of those. The plot is just empty-headed mush about a group of men who are trying to warn their buddy that he's falling for a woman who is, quite literally, a one-way ticket to hell.

Sort of like what we're going through now.

It's going to be awful if we're discovered and go into combat here, in front of our children.

Or worse yet, one of us gets shot.

I can feel my forehead dotting with perspiration as the men move up the aisle, closer and closer to us, swinging their flashlights into the glazed eyes of this full house of moviegoers. I think through our options. Maybe I'll fling the half-full cola cup from the guy beside me into the face of one of them, before taking him down with a few swift punches, then catapulting over the aisle and dashing out of the theater.

But that would mean leaving my children without any way to get them word as to why I've left, or what they should do next.

On the other hand, it's dark enough in here that maybe I can slide into a row with an empty seat, and maybe they'll—

"Kiss me," Jack commands.

"Really? This predicament is a turn-on for you?"

Obviously so, because the next thing I know his lips are on mine.

I should pull away and track the danger around us. Instead, I melt from the warmth of his kiss. My terror is eased by the familiar contours of his mouth and his playful tongue. He holds me gently in his arms, but his fingers roam, patting my hair before inching over my shoulders and onto my back, relaxing me into an embrace.

Through our kiss, we breathe, as if sharing one body.

When I look up, the flashlights of our would-be captors are a faint glow, receding toward the exit door.

For now, anyway.

Finally, when I catch my breath, I gasp, "Gee, I guess we fooled them."

The next kiss we share is fueled by the knowledge that *we're free.*

The lady behind us taps us on the shoulder. "Why don't you folks get a room?"

Jack's cell buzzes. He glances down at it and murmurs, "Not a bad idea. What would you say to a suite at the Sunset Tower?"

"But—we made it clear to Addison that we weren't interested."

"That's showbiz, babe. The word 'no' is catnip to a player like Addison. It means we're worth doubling down for."

"So now he's offered us *six thousand a day?*"

"Seems like it." He nods as he texts something. "If he comes up with a second suite, we'll say yes."

"Why do we need a second one?"

"For the kids—and Aunt Phyllis. Somebody has to watch over them while we make movie magic." A moment later, a text buzzes his cell. "He's agreed to the terms—which, by the way, include leaving you alone."

I blush. "You know, I'm quite capable of taking care of myself."

"That's why I keep you around—for my own protection." The only light in the theater is flickering off the screen. It's all I need to see his knowing grin.

"*Shhhhhh!*" The woman behind us has leaned so far forward that her face is now between us.

Jack takes it in both hands and plants a kiss on her lips.

At first she struggles, but she can't resist.

A moment later, he eases off, and she melts back into her seat with a sigh.

That's my boy.

Before I can say another word, he's off to wrangle the boys out of their seats. I do the same with the girls.

We're smart enough to wait until after we toss Morton and Cheever out of the car to tell the kids the exciting news:

For the next couple of weeks, they'll be enjoying room service at one of the ritziest hotels in Beverly Hills, while Jack 'consults on a film screenplay.'

In other words, while we rewrite our own Hollywood ending.

———————————————

6

The Last Tycoon

———————————————

"All writers are children. Fifty percent are drunks. And up until very recently, writers in Hollywood were gag-men. Most of them are still gag-men, but we call them writers."

Robert DeNiro, as "Monroe Stahr"

CUT TO:

EXT. HIGH-RISE ROOFTOP — DAY.

OUR HERO runs to escape three QUORUM HENCHMEN, all the while dodging the spray of BULLETS coming out of their AK-47s. When he reaches the edge, he looks over it —

To see a seven-story drop onto RAILROAD TRACKS.

SFX: TRAIN, now coming into sight and moving at bullet speed — so quickly, in fact, that the CABOOSE is already in view.

It's now or never. Our Hero takes a flying leap off the building —

And lands on top of the train, crouching, like a cat.

He looks up at the henchmen. Angrily, they shake their fists at him. Smiling, he rises triumphantly to his feet, and waves back.

CUT TO:

"LET ME GET THIS STRAIGHT—NEITHER OF YOU HAVE EVER jumped off the roof of a seven-story building, onto a moving train?" Justin DeVane may be a hipster screenwriter who wrote a Me Generation navel-gazing Sundance Film Festival Jury Recognition winner and parlayed that into a career as a script doctor, but the truth of the matter is that he's dumb as a post when it comes to physics.

Let alone any other science.

"Nope, not once," I assure him. "We're not cartoon road-runners, or super heroes. We're flesh and blood people. We'd slide off. As for that 'stands up triumphantly part,' in the real world, the centrifugal force would toss him off."

"You're quickly turning this movie into a downer." Stymied, Justin shakes his head. "Tell me, why are you here, again?"

Jack drops his head onto the screenplay placed on the table in front of him. This is the fiftieth time he's done that in the past twelve hours. Those one-hundred-and-ten pages of nonsense are the only things keeping him from getting a concussion. "Justin, in all honesty, we're here to save your ass on this picture."

"Alright already, I'll nix the moving train!" Justin frowns

as he considers his options. "Wait…I know! When he jumps, it'll be into the open window of the next building." His fingers are fast at work on his laptop computer.

I stand by the suite's open window—not because I'm going to jump just to prove the point, but because he is a chain smoker and I can't breathe. "Justin, you graduated from college, am I right?"

"Bennington."

Well, *la dee dah*. "Good! Then you've had at least a class or two in science." I plop down on a settee, which is in front of a coffee table holding a bowl of fruit. While my hands are busy slicing an apple with Jeff's Swiss army knife, my mind is measuring the distance between Justin and me for the ideal strike zone that would have him bleeding out the fastest.

Old habits die hard.

"I said *Bennington*—not MIT." His laugh becomes a raucous cough. I suppose that forty cigarettes a day will do that to you.

"Yes, of course. Silly me." I nod slowly, as if I'm talking to a first grader. "Okay, then a little lesson on aerodynamics is in order. You see, should a person leap off a building, their forward trajectory is, say, ten to fifteen feet at the most."

"Even someone in tip-top condition—say, an Olympic gold medalist in the running broad jump, can only go twenty-five, maybe twenty-eight feet, tops," Jack mutters from the table. "If you're talking about some flabby, middle-aged, overpaid actor who makes his living pantomiming stunts in front of a green screen, it's around seven feet— eight at best."

Justin shrugs. "They could always tie him to a tether, then CGI it out of there." He snaps his fingers. "Addison always hires the best stunt doubles. One of those guys could pull it off."

"No matter who jumps, or how far he jumps, his trajectory is still an arc—in other words, he may be moving forward for some of the journey, perhaps raising himself up by a foot or two." I try to talk to him as if he's Trisha—gently and sweetly, or as sweetly as I can between gritted teeth. "But Justin, no one falls *sideways*—and into an open window! Before he got there, he'd fall straight down. Newton called it 'gravity.'"

Justin throws up his hands. "Lady, it's a spy flick! If we were to portray what you really did—wait hours at dead drops, trail other spooks, listen in on mundane conversations, we'd leave audiences snoring—or even worse, walking out of theaters."

"You're not being fair. We've given you some great stuff," I counter. "Don't blame us if you keep falling back on the typical tropes: the horny rogue operative, the female desk op who's over her head when she's put out in the field—not to mention the villain who looks like a refugee from a clown college."

"Those of us who've won an Oscar, please raise your hand," Justin sneers.

"You've just made my point for me. Can't you be just a little bit more creative? Pretend the rewrite is more than just another paycheck. Create some cinematic art. My God, it's going to be in the hands of Scorsese, and starring Leo and

Amy. What will they think of this…"—I throw my copy of the screenplay on the table—"this dreck?"

He stares at me for a moment, then bursts out laughing. "I can understand Addison keeping you out of the loop, but don't you even read the trades? Scorsese passed, which means Leo and Amy did, too."

I can't believe my ears. "Then…who the hell is directing?"

"Addison has lined up Ben Affleck, so it's not a total wash." He winces. "And he's got Bradley Cooper as the lead. Jennifer Garner will be the love interest."

"Hmmm." Of course I'm disappointed that we've lost such a stellar director and leads, but that's no shabby punt, either. "That should work. It will bring in all the fans who remember them both from *Alias*—like some sort of reunion, with franchise potential. All good, right?"

"Oh, yeah, retro TV fans. All is *so* good." He doesn't even hide his smirk.

I stab another apple—perhaps a bit too hard, because the knife is now an inch deep into the table. I jerk it up with such force that the apple flies across the room, slamming into the wall with a loud splat.

Globs of apple pulp roll slowly to the floor.

However, the knife stays in my clenched fist. I shrug. "For once, I'd like to see a movie where at least one or two of the million bullets flying around actually wounds one of the good guys, too. How badly do you think trained assassins shoot, anyway?"

"I'm willing to bet you can't hit the side of a barn." Justin blows a perfect smoke ring in my direction.

My knife flies through the middle of it, and so close to his cigarette that he ducks.

His head hits the table.

Unfortunately, there's no script to cushion it. He's out like a light.

"What the hell, Donna?" Jack groans. "You're going to chase away this screenwriter, too?"

"Addison told us to be brutal. He wants the script as authentic as possible."

"He also said he needs it delivered by the end of the week, or else production is cancelled. If that happens, we lose this cozy little safe house." Jack reaches over to slap Justin's face, but this doesn't revive him. "Aw, what does it matter? One way or the other, the jig is up. The last two script doctors have already complained to the Writers Guild. If this one does, too, no one will touch the project no matter how much money Addison offers, and he'll have to shut down production, anyway."

"Maybe it's for the best. The kids are beginning to think that all meals should be served under sterling silver domes on room service trays." I walk to the window, where I have a bird's eye view of the hotel's terrace. "Can you believe it? Poor Mary can't catch a few rays by the pool without some guy trying to pick her up. Can't they see she's underage?"

"It doesn't help that she looks over-age in her bikini."

"I suggested a burqa. That recommendation went over like one of Morton's wet farts." I tap on the window, as if the man-boy leaning over my daughter is going to actually look up and see my scowl. I guess I'd have more clout if I'd kept the knife in my hand.

Before I can retrieve it from the pillow it has pinned to a wingback chair, Jack puts his arms around me. "She seems to be able to take care of herself."

He's right. Whatever she's said has the guy moon-walking away.

"She's depressed. I think she misses her friends. So do Jeff and Trisha."

"They stay in contact." He knows this because we've been monitoring their cell phone and iPad activity, as well as Mary's Facebook and Instagram accounts. Arnie was able to put GPS scramblers on our phones and all of our WiFi devices.

Mary lowers the brim of her sun hat and goes back to reading her iPad. I presume she's reading *Age of Innocence,* which is the lit homework due tomorrow. Through an untraceable server, I emailed all my children's teachers to tell them that we were taking a family sabbatical, but that our children would still be accountable for classwork.

Despite their parents' happy faces, my kids aren't dumb. They know there's something we aren't telling them.

I grab a broad-brimmed hat and my sunglasses and head down to the pool, so that I can get some fresh air.

Really, I need a hug. My guess is that Mary does, too.

THE POOL ON THE TERRACE LEVEL OF THE SUNSET TOWER IS THE place to see and be seen, especially on a beautiful afternoon.

Do my children recognize the many stars within spitting distance of them? My guess is no—unless they're wearing a super-hero costume, or still look as girlish or as boyish as they did in the teen movies they made just a few years ago.

Hanging by the pool days on end won't keep your skin forever twenty-one, but hanging by the Sunset Tower's pool says you've arrived.

Trisha splashes in the shallow end with the hotel's on-call au pair, a twenty-something adorable enough to have her own sitcom. But hey, in this town, the stardom competition is tough, to say the least. I don't envy the young and talented who stay to play, and certainly not those who are paid to pass.

While we're working, Aunt Phyllis supervises the children's studies. Afterward, she takes them on outings—to movies, the local parks and libraries, or the Farmer's Market.

When the kids hang at the pool, Aunt Phyllis parks herself in the hotel lobby with her knitting bag. From there, she can tune in on conversations. Lately she's been passing along gossipy tidbits to the TMZ hotline. It's one way of subsidizing a measly Social Security check. Or as she puts it, "No one expects the little old lady in the lobby to be their worst paparazzi nightmare."

Even Lassie and Rin Tin Tin have adjusted to hotel living. They sleep on little hotel beds, get walked in William S. Hart Park adjacent to the hotel, and enjoy the hotel's "pet dining menu," which includes chopped sirloin, grilled boneless chicken breast, and New York steaks, rare.

My youngest waves at me, but she's having too much fun pretending to be a porpoise to come over. I spot Jeff, sitting on a lounge chair that backs up to a cabana. He's writing furiously on his iPad. Without Morton and

Cheever to distract him, it seems he's become focused on his studies. At least one good thing has come from this situation.

I ease myself down onto the lounge chair beside Mary. "You're getting quite a tan."

She shrugs. Her eyes don't move from her book.

I try again. "Is that your assigned reading?"

She clicks off the iPad. "Mom, tell me the truth: why are we here?"

So much for small talk. I force my lips into a grin. "Don't you remember? Your father has been asked to consult on a movie script. The plot revolves around the banking industry."

She juts out her chin. Since she was two, this was the tell-tale that she doesn't like what she is hearing.

"Really? You expect me to believe that?"

I'll match her disbelief then raise it with my own tone of indignation. "What are you trying to say, Mary?"

"Babs texted me. She asked if I was upset—*about our house blowing up!* Mom, I didn't know how to answer her! You and Dad hadn't said anything. But you must have known about it…right?"

Ah, the moment of truth.

I nod. "We got the call from the fire department the afternoon we were at the movies."

Her anger propels her into an upright position. "You knew—but you didn't say anything?"

"Yes, we knew. But I didn't want you and Jeff and Trisha to be as upset over it as I am. And since we have to be here at the hotel anyway, I told your father I thought it would be best for us to settle in before we broke the news to the rest of the family."

Mary eases back into her chair. She lowers her sunglasses, revealing eyes that are red and rimmed with tears. I have no doubt she's thinking about the house, her room, and all of the things left behind that will no longer be a part of her life. "Is everything gone?"

"Sadly, yes. Nothing was saved."

"Will we ever move back?" she asks in a whisper.

"The insurers are assessing the damage now. Even if they do a full payout, the time and expense may not be worth it. On the other hand, since there hasn't been an empty lot in Hilldale for quite some time, it should go for a premium. It might be a better idea to sell it, as is."

She pulls away from me. "So your answer is no. We're never going back."

I place my hand over hers. "There's another reason why it's a very strong possibility that we won't be returning to Hilldale. Your father's company has offered him a transfer—out of the country. It means more money, and I guess it's one way to view our misfortune as a fresh start."

"But I don't need 'a fresh start.' I'd miss my friends! I like my teachers, and my school!"

I place my hand over hers. "What is truly important in our lives isn't things, or even places, but the memories we have, and the people who love us most, who have helped us create those memories. Mary, we're the most important people in each other's lives, aren't we?"

She nods. "Yes, of course."

"Should we make this move, we'll be sharing some invaluable experiences."

She doesn't say anything. Her eyes shift to our hands, mine over hers. "Mom, are you telling me everything?"

We tell our children that honesty is the best policy. And yet, when it comes to their wellbeing, the great parenting dilemma is deciding how, and when, we dole out information to them. Will what we tell them go over their heads? Worse yet, will it scare them? Will they understand our motives and respect our decisions?

Mary isn't an adult. She's no longer a child, either. She's right in pointing out that I owe her the truth, especially during these very crucial years in her life.

But she can't understand that the decisions we've made are not only on her behalf, but protect many innocent lives.

Jack's and my life depend on them, too. The next decision we make will determine our freedom.

All the more reason to squeeze her hands and say with all sincerity, "At this point, there is so much that neither your father nor I know. Mary, sweetheart, we're taking advantage of all the wonderful things coming our way."

She's about to say something when suddenly we hear some woman screaming, "Why, you little snoop! Give me that cell phone!"

The next thing I know, Jeff is running toward us. As he passes us, he drops his cell into Mary's beach bag, before bounding into the hedge behind us.

The woman comes out of a cabana on the far side of the pool. She's naked, except for the flimsy towel she's wrapping around herself. She stops when she sees us. "That boy —did you see him? Which way did he go?"

Mary and I stare at her, then at each other. We both point toward the elevator.

She runs off, tucking the towel around her as it slips.

I wait until we hear the elevator whisk her down into the hotel before grabbing Jeff's cell. I scroll through the photos he's taken—all of celebrities, who I guess had been hanging out, poolside, over the past few days.

Jeff pops out from behind a bush. "Is the coast clear?"

"For now," I say.

He flops down in the chair on the other side of Mary. But when he reaches for her bag, I grab his wrist with one hand. He looks up to see I'm holding his phone with the other.

"You know the hotel's policy. Why are you spying on these people?"

"Whenever I overhear something juicy, Aunt Phyllis cuts me in for some of her paparazzi fees."

"What? That's disgraceful!" I delete all the pictures.

Jeff folds his arms on his chest. "Why can't I help Aunt Phyllis? She needs me. Sometimes her hearing aid flakes out on her."

I shake my head firmly. "She's making enough now that she can afford a new one."

"Even if that's the case, she can't be in two places at once. She's already paid me twenty bucks for the leads I've picked up here, by the pool!"

"The money isn't the issue. Eavesdropping is hardly a profession. Worse yet, it isn't polite."

"Okay, whatever." But, by his scowl, I can tell he'll say anything to get me off his back.

Maybe I'm being too hard on him—really, on all of them. Although all the children haven't come out and said so, they know something isn't right with our little sabbatical. I've cut my hair shorter, and lightened it. Jack doesn't need them, but he's started to wear glasses anyway, parts his hair differently, and now sports a scruffy goatee. Whenever we go out in public, we wear sunglasses.

Aunt Phyllis teases us that we're "living like celebrities, and acting like them, too." She can think what she wants, just as long as she—or for that matter, the kids—don't realize the truth:

We've gone off the grid.

Well, a Hollywood version of it, anyway.

My children may not miss school, but they miss their friends and the continuity of their lives.

I hope they can soon get back to it.

If and when they do, it will be because Jack and I are sharing it with them.

7

Dead Poets Society

"Carpe diem. Seize the day, boys. Make your lives extraordinary."

Robin Williams, as "John Keating"

NOW THAT YOU HAVE YOUR INVITATION TO YOUR OWN MOVIE'S premiere in your gelled talons, of course you're wondering, "What will I wear?"

Hmmm. Great question—especially from someone who has worn the same ratty old jammies since high school. So that your promenade of fame doesn't turn into a walk of shame, here are three tips to avoid the typical fashion faux pas:

First, dress to compress. Any gown that puts you within spitting distance of your favorite movie stars is worth fighting the battle of the bulge. Just say "Spanx for the memories!"

Next, skip the train. The goal is to make it to your assigned seat without tripping on the hem of your gown. Forget the sky-

high heels and the too-long train and you can breeze in and smile pretty for the cameras.

Despite Diana Vreeland's fashion savoir faire, your first time on the red carpet is not the time to "give 'em what they never knew they wanted." Your very first time on the red carpet should not be an occasion for a nip slip or your thong doing you wrong, just because you packed your pistol in the wrong place. Better to avoid any dress that begs for a wardrobe malfunction.

Better yet, just this once, leave your gun at home.

You're just as lethal with your stiletto heel.

"WHAT'S IT LIKE TO WATCH SOMEONE DIE?" SEBASTIAN Gillingham, the latest and, so far, greatest screenwriter for *Lethal*, has waited to ask me this all day.

His timing is perfect. Just a moment ago I read the final page of his screenplay, and rewarded him two thumbs up—

Which is possibly why I'm spilling my drink all over the carpet.

Well, that and the fact I'm on my third tumbler of Bowmore. Whiskey isn't my usual cuppa, but this is a very expensive twenty-five year-old bottle of the stuff, so bottoms up, right?

We have a right to celebrate early. The screenplay is finally completed, and besides, happy hour started eons ago—

In Paris, if not Los Angeles.

Addison was lucky to get Sebastian on this project. In only four days, this award-winning screenwriter has done a wonderful job massaging *Lethal* into a thriller that is also a love story. The characters are no longer cardboard cutouts, but a man and a woman who must make life-or-death decisions and live with the consequences. The plot revolves around stolen intelligence. Its loss is the fault of the hero. The heroine holds the key, but she doesn't know it—yet. She once had a relationship with the villain—a terrorist who is both heartless and cunning. In reliving her feelings for him, will she fail in stopping him?

Sebastian has made Jack and my job easy. He graciously listened to our suggestions of how to make the scenarios of derring-do ring true, both in regard to the technical details and the emotions that drive them. Then, he just made a few simple changes—reworded a few lines of dialogue, or altered the action within the scene.

He has an Oscar on his mantle, but his cache of BAFTAs and Emmys comes from a BBC drawing room drama that's a hit on both sides of the pond.*Bloomsbury*, which dramatizes the life of Virginia Woolf, her sister Vanessa Bell, and other influential early twentieth-century writers, philosophers, and artists in her London social set, is being applauded for its attention to detail, nuanced performances and spot-on period dialogue.

No wonder word has it that Sebastian is a shoo-in for a knighthood, and not just because he's tall, elegant, and looks great in a tux.

His question not only catches me off-guard, it brings a blush to my cheeks, too. "I don't usually have the opportunity to hang around after a hit."

"Ah…yes, I imagine that would be the case." He laughs

at his own naïveté. His bashfulness is part of his charm. In fact, he's so shy that he has never looked me in the eye—yet another of his many endearing traits. "But the way you've described your hits to me—how you research your targets, how you get close to them without their even noticing you're there, that you even know them intimately—I would think that you'd feel some sort of…I don't know. Perhaps the word I'm looking for is—"

"The word I think you mean is remorse. By the time their name is on my to-do list, they've already been very bad boys —or, for that matter, girls."

"But they have lives. Maybe even spouses and children." He tosses back his head, so that his bangs stay out of his eyes. It's a nervous habit. Despite being in his forties, he still wears his hair as if he's in his third year at Oxford.

Or perhaps he thinks women find it adorable.

I'm a woman, and yes, it has its allure.

Jack, on the other hand, finds it annoying. But what he finds even more irritating is Sebastian's subtle attempts to veer us away from the technical aspects of our job by tossing in a question or two about our personal lives.

I'm sure it's why Jack passed on this little celebration, claiming he had "another appointment." In truth, he's out walking the dogs, but I don't dare tell Sebastian that Jack prefers their company to his.

Right now, I can't say I blame Jack. This question certainly gives me reason to pause. "In most cases, yes. They have lives beyond their day jobs as terrorists. But it hasn't stopped them from ruining the lives of others."

"But isn't terrorism in the eyes of the beholder?" Sebastian pours yet another two fingers of Bowmore into his glass. Ever the thoughtful guest, he splashes my tumbler, too. Okay, more than a splash. Enough so that even Jack's rudeness no longer bothers me.

I don't want to lose the giddiness of our success, so I tap the rim of my glass to his. "What do you mean by that?"

"One man's terror attack is another's fight for freedom."

I shake my head adamantly. "Terrorism is not a political statement. It's a bullying tactic used against the defenseless. It ruins the lives of families who just want to get on with their daily, ordinary lives. They kill families in local shopping malls, and children on soccer fields. The average John and Jane Doe having lunch in a coffee shop may have the bad fortune of standing next to a suicide bomber when he blows sky high. I can tell you unequivocally that terrorism is not how you win friends and influence voters. If you want to make your case, you do it at the ballot box. Trust me, the terrorists know this."

Sebastian's frown is evidence of his disbelief. "In your country, big business lobbies for what it needs. It also buys public opinion. What about John and Jane Doe then? Who looks after them?"

"Sometimes, the task falls to me." I tap the screenplay with my index finger. "You've got some of what we do right here. If only I were as gorgeous as Jennifer Garner."

Sebastian winces. "Or whomever."

I choke on my whiskey. "What do you mean by that?"

"She dropped out, right after her husband pulled out of directing it."

"Let me guess—Cooper is out, too."

"Seems like it, unless Addison can coerce Jennifer Lawrence to take the role. When it comes to leads, those two are practically joined at the hip." He taps the script, too. "After reading this, she'd be a fool to pass, if I do say so myself."

"I agree." I try to stand up, but I'll admit it—I'm a bit tipsy.

Ever the gentleman, Sebastian puts his arm out to steady me.

Instead, I end up in his lap.

"Sorry! I guess I've had too much to drink."

"Not to worry," he smiles, as if it were the most natural thing in the world that I'd end up there.

As quickly as I can, I leap—okay, make that fall—out of his lap. He stands up in order to reach down to help me up—

Instead he ends up on the floor beside me.

We both laugh at this. At first, we exchange embarrassed chuckles, but soon we're into full-blown snorting, to the point that we're both rolling on the carpet.

Face down, I gasp, "My God, I don't remember the last time I just let loose like this!"

I turn my head toward Sebastian to find him staring at my backside. When our eyes meet, he smiles. Picking up the whiskey bottle, he murmurs, "Bottoms up."

"Um…I don't think I should drink anymore."

I rise to my knees, but slowly, because I'm woozy. I don't want to throw up on the carpet. The dogs would think I'd left them a treat, and the next thing I know, I'd be cleaning up after them instead.

Ugh. Can't stand up. I settle back down onto my knees again. Sort of. More like yoga. Downward dog. Good, the blood is rushing to my head. Much better. Yes, exercise will do me good.

No, vomit rushing there, too. I collapse into the cobra position: on my stomach, head and shoulders lifted.

Sebastian is sitting on the bed, albeit he's not half as looped. What's he reading? Is that the Gideon's Bible from the night table? "You like to journal, do you?"

I'd try nodding, but in this position, I'd only be asking for trouble. I don't want to pull a Linda Blair. "Yes. Old habit. It's for my children…when they're old enough to understand why I do…you know, my job."

"Totally understandable." He flips the pages. "I'm old enough, though. You don't mind, do you? It may help me find the key as to why I find you so beguiling."

He finds me beguiling?

Hmmmm.

But no. "No…" Sorry, I can't let you read it, Sebastian. What I write is personal, and for my eyes only. My God, even Jack has never seen my journals.

Not yet.

Ouch! My head hurts…

Closing my eyes makes it better.

So. Does. Sleep.

HE'S KISSING ME.

"Sebastian—no!" I smack him away.

He nips my hand and growls. Talk about crossing the line—

Only it's not Sebastian. It's Rin Tin Tin.

I roll over to find Jack, staring down at me.

I stumble to my feet. "Where's…"

"Sebastian? I have no idea. I've just returned with the dogs." He picks up the empty whiskey bottle on the floor beside me. "It must have been quite a party."

"You could have stayed, you know. In fact, we were just waiting for you to come back. He offered to take us all to dinner." Damn it, I wish Jack would quit moving. I didn't know he had a twin…

He steadies me with both hands on my arms. "I would have passed. You know what they say, 'three's a crowd.'"

"Don't be jealous!"

"I'm not. Frankly, I think it's hilarious that you're star struck."

"I am not! Besides, he's a writer, not an actor."

"He's got an Oscar, and he speaks the King's English as if he were the King. Admit it, Donna: if he was from Oxford, Mississippi, as opposed to Oxford, England, would you be batting your lashes at him?"

"If I bat my lashes—and I'm not admitting to it—perhaps it's because he finds me 'beguiling,'" I counter. "They don't use words like that in Mississippi."

"You're right. He would have called them 'tah-tah's.' Doesn't have the same ring to it at all."

"What are you implying?"

"I'm not. I'm stating a fact. Have you noticed that he

never looks you in the eye? He can't tear himself away from staring at your breasts."

"Oh! …Well, that's beside the point."

"No, it's exactly"—he looks at my breasts, and smiles —"the points."

I slam the bedroom door and lock it behind me.

He can sleep on one of the hotel's doggy beds with Rin Tin Tin and Lassie, as opposed to in here, with "the points"—Pixie and Dixie—and me.

Lovely, lovely, everything is *so* lovely at the Ivy on North Robertson!

Our thank-you-and-farewell lunch (wild lobster salad for me, a Kobe-style New York Steak for Jack—on Addison's dime of course) is being served on the terrace, under a sun-kissed baby blue sky. Vines of yellow roses coil around the white picket fence in the front. The brick walls on either side are adorned with green boxes of hot pink geraniums.

Addison and Sebastian sit on green wrought-iron chairs, leaving the white wicker settee lined with colorful floral, paisley, and gingham pillows for Jack and me. This suits me fine because it allows me to take quick glances at all the actors, directors and various Hollywood movers and shakers sitting at the tables around us. Yes, that is Cate Blanchett in the corner, and I've just knocked elbows with Robert Downey, Jr. (or RDJ as his friends call him) apologizes to me. (To me! *Me!* Squeeee! Oh my goodness, he's got the bluest eyes…)

Between chitchat about the projects of the various players around us, Addison and Sebastian have been singing our praises. (Can RDJ hear them? Is that why he turns to smile at me? *Me! Squeeee!*)

Damn, I wish Jack would at least pretend to listen to our hosts! Instead, his eyes are constantly on the move. Why is he so distracted by all the cars that pass the restaurant? Robertson is a four-lane road, for goodness sake! If he's not noting every drop-off at the valet stand, he scans the faces around us—not because he's star struck, but out of boredom, I presume.

He's ignoring me, too. Noticing Bryan Cranston *not three feet away from us*, I squeeze Jack's hand to get his attention. Finally he tears himself away from his pouting to see what I want. I nod in the direction of this ultimate celebrity sighting. All I get for my troubles is a squeeze back—

One that hurts.

To retaliate, I pinch him—hard.

He curses loud enough that Sebastian stops what he's saying—some little anecdote about him and Benedict Cumberbatch at the soiree for Royal Academy of Dramatic Arts at Buckingham Palace.

Jack is so rude.

Not to mention that he's barely touched his steak. That's okay. I'll get it put in a doggy bag. Not really for the dogs, of course, but for the rest of us. Now that we've vetted the script, I'm sure this will be the last decent meal we'll be having for a very long time. Drive-through McDonald's Happy Meals aren't exactly lobster salad with the stars, but it's all you get when you're on the lam.

With all the flowery compliments coming out of Addison's mouth, I'm sure he wouldn't mind if I ordered a few more entrees and took them to go. Yummy, the spicy chicken gumbo ya-ya looks delicious…Oh look, it's what RDJ ordered! Now that we're practically besties, I wonder if he'd let me sample a bite—

"—franchise potential, which would mean ongoing consulting for you." Addison declares.

"Seriously?" Tah-tah to the ya-ya. It's time to talk turkey. "Why, that would be wonderful!" I elbow Jack. "Don't you think so, dear?"

"Yeah, sure, whatever." He's still got his eyes peeled to the sidewalk traffic. What the heck is wrong with him?

"In fact, we'd like you on the set as well, through the whole six-week shoot," Addison continues. "Immediately, in fact." He pauses. "Of course, we'll first have to get both of you to sign off on the script changes Sebastian has proposed, now that it's based on your life story."

The lobster shell cracker falls out of my hand and onto my plate with a crash. "Our…*what?*"

Finally Addison has our undivided attention—which, from the looks on our faces, is not necessarily a good thing.

Realizing this, he positions himself to give his best elevator pitch for this ludicrous idea. "Didn't Sebastian mention it? Apparently he feels the information he found in *Donna*'s personal journals"—he emphasizes my name, now that he's discovered I'm not Jane Smith—"would give the plot and story a whole new dimension. How did you put it, Sebastian? Oh yeah! You said, 'We feel her pain.'" He puts a hand on the screenwriter's shoulder.

They *do?*

They like me. They really, really like me…

"Her personal journals?" Jack looks at me as if he's seeing me for the very first time. "You mean, her cookbooks?"

I force a smile on my face as I turn to face Jack. "Honey, those aren't exactly cookbooks. I mean, yes, they are cookbook *binders*, but the pages inside are some personal notes I've made."

He blinks hard. "You mean, all the time we've been together, you weren't just jotting down *recipes?*"

"Well, yes of course I've got my favorites in there—and my mother's, too. But I also write about…I guess about my life." Just like a man, not to notice the things that mean the most to the love of his life! My God, how many recipes does he think I know?

And just like a man to read something personal without a proper invitation. I shift my glare to Sebastian. "How dare you! Who gave you permission to read them?"

"Why, you, my dear! Don't you remember?"

"No!" Boy, do I have a headache. Okay, yes, let's call it what it is—a hangover. "Perhaps I had a bit too much to drink."

Sebastian sighs. "You Americans. You should learn to hold your liquor." He takes my hand. "Donna, you're absolutely right to keep a diary. You're living an incredible story —one that will enthrall audiences all over the world—"

"You've got that right," Addison chimes in. "It'll be bigger than the Bond franchise! Sebastian spent all night beefing up the new script with your backstories. In fact, he's already put together a six-movie arc. The family angle adds depth and dimension. And the grudge match between you and this Carl guy is the crux of the story—"

I stand up, indignant. "What do you mean, the 'grudge match is the real story?' My betrayal is what this is about, and how I avenge what I presume is a wrong—"

"It doesn't matter what any of you think because the damn thing won't see the light of day." Jack's tone is hard as steel. "It can't. Much of what she's written about is classified intel."

The faintest of smiles rises on Sebastian's lips. "How do you know? You've just admitted you haven't read it."

Jack's face turns red. His eyes narrow as he turns to me. "Just what, exactly, do those journals contain, Donna?"

"Well…" I have to word this carefully. It's true my diaries contain information on missions that are classified, not to mention a few things the kids might find embarrassing. At the same time, who wouldn't want to see their life portrayed on the big screen—by Jennifer Lawrence, no less! "Jack, in all honesty, there's really nothing in there that can't be tweaked."

He leans back, glowering. "So, there's no mention of Breck?"

I gulp hard. "I didn't say that."

"How about the other Quorum members?"

I pause.

Gee, I wish I could say the same about Sebastian. He exclaims, "The way Acme ensnared them is sheer genius! Of course, what makes the plot even more thrilling is how, at each turn, you're stymied by your nemesis—because of this marvelous woman sitting in front of us! In fact, I've proposed that the title be changed from *Lethal* to *The House-wife Assassin's*...oh, bloody hell, I don't know. What do you think of 'Handbook'?" His epiphany has him all smiles. "My God, that's brilliant! *The Housewife Assassin's Handbook!*"

"I can think of another name for it," Jack mutters. "How about *The Convicted Housewife?*"

He's got a point, since our nemesis *is now the head of the US intelligence community.* Can't forget that little detail, now can we?

"Sorry, boys, our story isn't for sale," Jack stands up, pulling me with him. "You'll have to go back to the script we approved."

The color drains out of Addison's face. "Wait! I'm open to negotiation. How about a hundred thou for the rights to your life story?"

Now, I'm insulted, too. I stand up. "Really? Is that all you think I'm worth?"

But before I can say another word, Jack yanks me back down on the settee.

Make that under the table.

"What the hell do you think you're doing?" I whisper.

He puts his finger to his lips, to silence me. "Saving our lives. There are three NSA agents on the street, checking out the tables."

Oh, hell. "How did they know we were here?"

"Great question. An even better one is how are we going to get out of here?"

"We can't have a shoot-out!" Real blood—on real actors?

I can see the headline in *Hollywood Reporter* now: "Housewife Assassin Slays Hollywood Elite."

"You're right Donna—it's an insult," Addison says from above. "But—but please, no rough stuff!" Addison must have heard me say "shoot-out" and thinks we're talking about him, because his voice is quivering. "What say we make it a quarter-mil?"

I raise my hand beyond the table and let my middle finger do the talking for us.

Jack slaps my hand until I lower it again. He points under the tablecloth, where we can see three pairs of highly polished black wingtips under crisply creased black suit pants walk past the table, stop, and then scatter in pairs, over the terrace.

"Alright! Half a mil," Addison pleads, "and, of course, you'll be executive producers."

"I take a sheet of paper from my purse and scribble something, then raise my hand in order to slap it on the table.

"What? A million, and a gross point—apiece? Are you crazy?"

Jack and I stay silent as the black wingtips congregate in front of RDJ's table for a recon confab. "Dudes, do you mind?" The star's exasperated tone does the trick. They head back out onto the street.

A moment later, we hear their SUV peel off.

Addison must think our silence is a negotiating tactic because he's quiet, too, but his foot is twitching. Good. That'll teach him not to lowball the next sap. Finally he says,

"Yeah, okay, it's a deal. But you have to be ready to leave tonight, for our first location shoot—in Turkey."

I stick my head up. "Why there?"

"It boils down to dollars and cents. Turkey is a cheap place to shoot. We'll spend pennies on every dollar we would have spent anywhere else."

"I don't like it," Jack mutters to me. "And neither will Ryan."

"We don't have a choice!" I counter. "We have to get out of the country, and fast."

He sighs. He knows I have a point.

I follow him as he crawls out from under the table.

"Send the Final Draft version to this email. If we can live with the bulk of it, we'll make edits as we see fit. Let me make this clear: any attempts at unapproved changes during production, the deal is off." Jack scribbles down what looks like an innocuous gmail address. In truth, it's routed through a fake IP address coming from a masked browser, which has a custom firewall that not only protects against hacking, but also allows us to worm our way into the hacker's computer.

In this case, any version of the script we don't like is toast. "And, by the way, Bradley Cooper looks nothing like me," Jack mutters.

The producer laughs. "No need to worry there. He passed on the project."

My heart sinks. "So, I guess this means J Law is out, too. Am I right?"

"Donna darling, not to worry! I know you'll be beside yourself as to who plays you, but I want to keep you in suspense until we're wheels-up tonight and I have both stars already signed, sealed and delivered. But just to whet your appetite, I'll let you in on a little secret! We've got Reed Horwitch to play Handsome, here." He nods toward Jack.

Tall, dark, and hunky, sure, but Reed Horwitch is a sitcom actor with limited range—and from what I've read in the tabloid press, a truly obnoxious horn dog. I'll break this news to Jack later—when we're on the plane, and there's no turning back.

Then again, do I really want to be forty thousand feet up in the air if he doesn't like what I have to say?

I'll have to take that chance.

"A gentleman never reads a lady's diary," I mutter to Sebastian as we walk away from the table.

"You'll forgive me when you read it." He grins assuredly at me. "And by the way, you'll be stunning on the red carpet, my dear."

He's playing me and we both know it.

I'm not worried about tripping the light fantastic. It'll be a miracle if this movie gets made.

"So, what do you think?" I ask Jack as I click the SEND button, transmitting our vetted version of the screenplay to Ryan, so that he can weigh in on it, too.

Jack doesn't say a word. He just sits there, deep in thought.

Five minutes go by. I can't stand it anymore. "Please Jack, say something."

He sighs, but doesn't move. Finally, he shrugs. "It's in Sebastian's favor that he focused on the love story."

"I think so, too." Because it's *our story*—about two people who are thrown together under terrible circumstances. They must work as a team. But, can they really trust each other?

The script is now true to life.

Maybe too true.

I feel the heroine's pains, because they are also mine.

And I know Jack relates to the hero, perhaps too much.

His computer screen shows his edits and mine, side by side. A faint smile rises on his lips. "I guess we're of like mind as to the changes that must be made."

"Then we'll say yes to Addison?"

"A million bucks goes a long way to assuaging my concerns." He pulls me onto his lap. "Of course, Ryan has the last word. If I were you, I wouldn't get my hopes up."

"You're probably right." I try not to show my disappointment. "Well, at least we've already earned a few shekels to float us for the next month or so, especially if we go off the grid."

He laughs. "Talk about a culture shock for the kids!" His grin disappears. "Donna, I'd like permission to read your diaries. I know they were originally meant for your eyes only, so if you feel it's an intrusion, I'll thoroughly respect your answer either way—"

I put my fingers to his lips. "I've been waiting two and a half years for you to ask."

He blinks. "Really?"

"Yes, really." I lay my hand in his. "I'm no fool. I realize any day may be my last. And I'm fully aware that others—

especially Carl—will do what they can to discredit me. I started my little 'handbook' because I wanted the children to know, from me, why I chose the path I've taken. It proves I love them—and you—more than life itself." My tears are dropping fast now.

He takes a finger and nudges them off my cheek.

I take his finger and kiss it gently.

He takes this as my tacit approval to kiss the palm of my hand. Soon his hand has moved up my arm, onto my neck.

Until his lips meet mine.

It's easy to get lost in a kiss.

I break the spell it has cast over us by pressing him down onto the couch.

He has already hardened. He groans as I ease myself onto him.

As we find our tempo, my mind ricochets between two emotions: from the joy surging through me—right here, right now—to my irrational fear of his response to what he reads.

Baring my body to him is one thing. Baring my soul is quite another.

Our orgasms tremble through us, twin thunderbolts that shock and surge and charge before subsiding in our spent bodies.

I don't know how long I've slept in his arms before he gently nudges me into the crux of the couch and heads off to the shower.

I am blissfully sated, but famished just the same. "I'll order room service," I call out to him.

"Tell them to hurry," he shouts from the bathroom.

"Why? We don't have to leave for at least another three hours."

He peeks out from the shower door. "My point exactly."

I put in an order for two steaks and mashed potatoes.

Oh yes, and chocolate sauce.

"Skip the ice cream," I tell Room Service.

Jack is dessert.

SOMETHING ABOUT THE ROOM SERVICE WAITER WHO HAS brought in our dinner cart looks oddly familiar. Jack is still in the shower, so I can't signal him to be on his guard. Instead, I smile and show the man in, motioning him toward the dining area. "Put it over there. I'll be right back with your tip."

He nods, but doesn't speak.

Because he's afraid I'll recognize his voice.

The dining area is a good fifty feet from the front door. If he's got my skill set, he'll know he has to take the creaking cart all the way into the room before easing his gun out from wherever he hid it. (*Is it under the tented napkin, or under the entrée dome? Does he have it strapped to his back? Eeny meeny miney mo…*)

In the meantime, I grab the letter opener off the desk. After today's run-in with the Feds, I can't take any chances. If anything, we can use him as a hostage.

I slip behind him, close enough that I'm out of his peripheral vision. When he finally stops I jab him hard—in the kidney, with my fist. The pain causes him to groan. Instinctively he reaches for his back. A moment later, I've wrenched one of his arms behind his back—

But he freezes when he feels the letter opener I'm holding under his throat.

"Don't hurt me." The plea comes out in a whisper. "It's…Arnie!"

Slowly, I lower the letter opener. Arnie collapses onto the cart.

"May I ask why you felt the need to carry on your charade beyond our doorstep?" I ask him.

"I guess it was a stupid idea. I just wanted to try out a new disguise." He points at his face. "Brown contact lenses, the 'stache, the blond wig and the sixties eyeglasses." Arnie lifts up the domes of our dinner trays to see what goodies we've ordered.

I shrug. "To be honest, it sucks. I can see the contacts through your glasses. No one needs both, right? Oh, and next time, make sure the lenses in your glasses have some wave to them so they look real. Also, the 'stache sags on one side." I pat his belly. "One last thing: this ain't no Trave-Lodge. A classy joint like this would never let you out of the employee locker room with a uniform that's obviously too tight around the gut."

He lowers the dome with a scowl. "Since when did you become so observant?"

"Being at the top of Interpol's Wanted Persons list will do that to a person." I shrug. "So, to what do we owe the plea-sure of your company?"

He lifts up the lid on the smallest dish. "Underneath are two iPhones. "Emma is monitoring the NSA's chatter on you and Jack. They think you're still somewhere in the LA metro area. Just in case, these are equipped with a new type of GPS scrambler, which puts you a country or two away from wherever you're standing."

"I thought I heard a familiar voice." Jack is at the bathroom door. He's wrapped in a bathrobe. His hair is damp and slicked back. "How are things back in the real world?"

Arnie tears into one of our rolls. Through a mouthful of bread, he says, "I got the thumbs-up on the tech advisor position on the production crew, but they're waiting for final script approval. And now we've got it—at least, as far as Ryan is concerned. He felt you both did a great job in vetting it for any recognizable issues."

Jack is frowning as he grabs a roll. "He's the boss," he mutters as he butters it. He still has issues with making our lives public. No surprise there.

"In fact, Ryan sees several advantages to signing off on the project. Obviously, the money is a big part of it. The second is that it gets you out of the country as soon as possible. Besides, if people know the real story, maybe we can swing public opinion in our favor, and the Feds will back off."

Jack gives Arnie a grudging nod. He knows Ryan is right on all three counts. Today's close call with the NSA is proof.

"By the way, I passed Ryan this list of shooting locations." Arnie pulls out a printout and hands it to me.

"You mean, we won't just be in Turkey?"

"Turkey is out altogether," he says. "Venezuela is in—and just for the Hilldale—excuse me, I mean 'Springfield' interior scenes." Arnie stuffs another roll into his mouth. If he starts on the mashed potatoes, he's a dead man. "We're shooting on a small island off the Venezuelan coast. It's called Isla Margarita."

"Why there?" I ask.

"In the first place, it's close to the US. Also, Addison can rent a whole resort for pennies on the dollar. And with all that's going on down there right now, the government is too preoccupied to snoop around," Arnie explains. "At the same time, it welcomes Montague Studios with open arms. *Mucho bolivars*, eh?" Arnie rubs the thumb and forefinger of his right hand against each other.

"That makes sense," Jack reasons. "And Venezuelan citizens are more concerned about their civil liberties than about a bunch of American actors shooting an inane movie."

I jab Jack in the ribs. "Hey! The script is sensitive—and true to life—and—"

"Yeah, yeah, whatever," he smirks. "Just keep telling yourself that."

"And besides," Arnie adds, "Serena LaCosta is living there now. Ryan is hoping she's grateful enough that you saved her that she may be willing to speak out on Donna's behalf regarding Carl's assassination of both Antoinette and Jonah Breck."

Serena LaCosta was another Hilldale nanny whom Jonah Breck seduced, then sent to the island in order to be raped and snuffed. Thanks to Jack, Carl never knew she was there when he eliminated Jonah and Antoinette.

"Then production moves to a couple of other locales: Paris, then London. Interestingly enough, each of these locations brings us closer to proving to President Chiffray that

Carl must be put behind bars. Dominic is already in London, chasing down an asset who can verify Carl's role in the murder of a German diplomat. In the meantime, Abu is following up on the lead we have in France—a former Quorum agent who worked closely with Carl. We don't know much about it, but we'll have more intel on him soon. Abu will be shadowing the production so that he can work the field for the assets in question." Arnie lifts the lid on the potatoes, but when he sees the look in my eyes, he drops it. Good boy.

Jack nods. "With Abu there, we'll have another set of eyes and ears in the field, if need be."

Arnie pushes up the droopy side of his mustache. I guess it finally bothers him as much as it bothers me. "Another piece of good news! I got Emma a job on the crew, as a make-up assistant."

"That's great," I say, "But will it give Emma enough time to help you with all the ComInt coming in?"

"Knowing her, she'll be fine." Even as he says this, Arnie turns red. Only Ryan is oblivious that the two of them are an item.

If only Arnie would move it in the right direction—toward the altar.

Maybe a few exotic locales will put him in the right mindset.

I've no doubt it will do wonders for Jack and me.

8

Body Double

"I do not do animal acts. I do not do S&M or any variations of that particular bent, no water sports either. I get two thousand dollars a day and I do not work without a contract."

Melanie Griffith, as "Holly Body"

Isn't it exciting? You've been invited onto a movie set! So that the experience of seeing your favorite actors up close and personal will be memorable for all the right reasons, keep these three simple rules in mind:

First off, don't act like a fan. In other words, when you recognize a movie star, don't (a) scream, (b) point, (c) faint, (d) stutter, (e) laugh hysterically, or (f) cry uncontrollably.

If you do, you'll just (a) look like a fool, (b) be treated like the village idiot, or (c) be escorted off the lot by security personnel.

Next, don't be shocked if the actor you love in all her roles doesn't live up to your expectations. Accept the fact that she'll have wrinkles, bad breath, an attitude, won't give a damn as to whom you are, and will call security if you try to pet her, no matter how gently. Bottom line: they're as human as the rest of us, not some animal in a star-studded zoo.

And finally, don't play with the props—especially on the set of a thriller. Since no one gave you a peek at the script, you don't know if something is rigged to emit a puff of smoke that will later be computer-generated to look like an explosion, or if some pyrotechnics will take place and blow you sky high.

And no, you're not doing the director a favor by substituting your gun for the fake prop one, "just to add realism."

MY CHILDREN ARE HIDING UNDER A BED WHILE BAD GUYS swarm our house looking for them.

My stomach is queasy, for all the wrong reasons. First off, they aren't really my kids, just actors hired to play them in a movie. The bad guys are actors, too, and when you meet them, you realize they aren't so menacing. They're just a bunch of happy ripped and cut cabana boys from Venezuela —the first stop on our three-country whirlwind production schedule.

The production company has rented out a private resort on Isla Margarita. This tiny island is located just northwest of the mainland, but still within a short boat ride to Caracas, Venezuela's capital.

The accommodations are luxe. The main building—a four-story hotel designed like an 1800s plantation house, has humongous rooms, which easily accommodate several cameras, the vast undulating cast and crew, and the sets that mimic the interiors found in a typical California suburban home. Besides the home interiors, there is also a schoolroom, a generic corporate office, the villain's hideout and yes, even a fake Starbuck's interior.

Here on the island, the breezes are warm and salty. The sand is white and powdery. The waves are sluggish and tepid.

Each of the lead actors has a private cabana, facing the resort's private beach.

The family Stone has one too. At night, while the children sleep to the endless lullaby of Aunt Phyllis's gentle snores, Jack and I go skinny-dipping in the lazy surf. We've only been here a week, but already I feel the anxiety drifting off my shoulders, like dry sugary sand on gently sun-kissed skin.

On the other hand, the crew fidgets anxiously while waiting for their star, who is still MIA:

Fake Donna Stone.

Today, still no star in sight.

In the meantime, the film's director, Whitford Fuller, shoots around her. Most of the scenes in which the children are by themselves have been shot, as have close-ups of the children, "John Smith," and anyone else who has one in the film. Some of the action shots utilizing the stunt doubles are also in the can.

Per our contract, on the set and in the movie we are to be referred to as John and Jane Smith. Also in regard to the movie, our children's names are Dick, Jane and Sally.

In this scene, just when Dick, Jane and Sally think the coast is clear, an arm reaches under the bed and grabs the leg of the youngest, Sally, pulling her out of her hiding place. "Sally" lets loose with a bloodcurdling scream.

"Cut!" yells Whitford. "Okay, kids! You're excused for the rest of the day. Go play on the beach. Even better, go run lines for tomorrow's scenes." He rubs the weariness from his eyes. It's only two in the afternoon, but already it's been a long day. "As for the crew, they finally get to set up for our beloved lead actress, who I hear will be flying in at any moment now." He waves toward the mansion. "Let's get the boudoir scenes between Mr. and Mrs. Smith out of the way first!"

"All five of them at once, boss?" The head grip scratches his head, puzzled.

Whitford sighs. "Yeah, well, this is one area in which our leading lady is actually a gifted pro, so it shouldn't take us too long to shoot."

Snickers can be heard throughout the sound stage.

"What does he mean by that?" Emma asks the wardrobe mistress.

"She used to do…well, let's just say she's a method actress from Chatsworth." The woman, Leda Smathers, laughs raucously. "This afternoon should be interesting, to say the least. Reed Horwitch may be an amateur, but he's 'gifted,' too." She holds her hands apart by about a foot.

Emma blushes, and I know why. Reed has been flirting with her from the moment he plopped down into her make-up chair.

As fascinated as my children are with the production, I

know where they will be for the rest of the afternoon: *anywhere but here.*

Addison has been reluctant to come forward with who is actually playing me in the film. In fact, he has sworn the cast and crew to secrecy, warning them that they'll be docked a week's worth of pay if they mention or spread rumors as to whom she is, so my snooping has turned up bupkis.

When I ask him why he can't reveal who she is, even to me, he opens his arms wide. "I don't want it leaked until she arrives with the reporter from *Variety*, since I promised that rag the scoop."

Oh my God! She must be someone huge.

Trisha stares at Darla Hood, the nine-year-old starlet who plays her in the movie. Noting my youngest daughter's fascination, Darla comes over to say hello. "So, how did I do?"

"Okay…I guess," Trisha says. She hesitates, then adds, "But you don't really look like me."

"Sure I do, only I'm smarter and cuter." Darla blows a perfect nicotine vapor smoke ring high above Trisha's head before turning off her electronic cigarette. Seems that Darla is practicing smoking for her next film, an eighties-era coming-of-age tween flick that, at least according to her mother, Darla Senior, will be her "breakout film."

Trisha's tiny hands curl into fists. "I don't think you're prettier! Frankly, I think you're too old!"

Darla laughs raucously. "Don't tell my agent, or my career will be over." She nods over toward the craft table. "Come with me, kid. There's a doughnut over there with your name on it."

Trisha's eyes open wide at the smorgasbord of goodies. "Really? Is that for me, too?"

Darla shrugs. "Someone's got to eat it. Heck, I can't. I've got to keep my girlish figure. And all the other stars have personal chefs preparing customized meals for their special dietary needs. So, you might as well not let it go to waste." She takes Trisha's hand and walks her over.

I'd object to Trisha chowing down on sweets so early in the morning, but why ruin her bonding moment with her doppelganger?

My children are thrilled that they're "consulting" on the movie with the actors portraying children who are supposed to be their actual ages. But what they find hilarious is that the movie family has parents who are spies.

"The mommy should be a housewife like you," Trisha points out to me. "Spies are always in danger. If anything happened to her, the children would be sad."

"I'll tell the director that she should never get hurt," I promise to my youngest.

It's the same vow I plan on keeping for myself.

I'm relieved Jeff has little interest in hanging with Mickey Daniels, the actor playing the Smith boy, Dick, in the movie. As it turns out, my son would much rather be shadowing Whitford and Addison. As the camera rolls, he sticks close enough to Whitford to be his shadow, watching his every move, especially his directions to the cameramen and the cinematographer.

On the other hand, Mickey may be short and slight, but the fact that the make-up crew has to cover up the stubble on his upper lip means he's already gone through puberty, and all that implies.

He keeps making plays at Mary, but she won't give him the time of day. She's having too much fun running lines and hanging out with Fake Mary—really, Rachel Garland, an actress who just turned twenty, and I'm happy to report, seems sweet and level-headed. She is polite to the crew, doesn't drink or smoke, does yoga and sticks to a vegetarian diet. No wonder the press has crowned her "Hollywood's Sweetheart."

"Mom, when Rachel was ten, she put together a list of all the directors she wanted to work with before she reached thirty. She's already made films with six of them," Mary says, awed. "I feel like such a slacker."

I pat her head. "Don't be so hard on yourself. Not everyone realizes their passion at such a young age."

She frowns. "Still, now that I'm in high school, I should be thinking about the future, about what I really want to accomplish in my life."

"You're right. High school is a great time to begin setting goals, and to have new experiences. But know that, at any point, you don't have to stick to something if it doesn't feel right. Sometimes the right opportunity presents itself when you least expect it, and sometimes life deals you a different hand than you'd like."

I speak from experience.

Rachel waves Mary over, and the two girls are off and running. When they're not on the set, they seem to be within chatting distance of Sebastian.

"It's all part of Rachel's long-term plan," Mary explained.

"She told me that great roles start with great writers. She wants to impress him enough that he'll write her into *Bloomsbury*."

I can see why Rachel is already turning heads in Hollywood. If Sebastian doesn't quite see her potential yet, I have no doubt she'll find a way to make him change his mind.

It's between takes on the first day of filming. Counting cast and crew, there are almost three hundred people here on location. Another two hundred-plus hearty souls are involved in either pre- or postproduction.

But from what I can tell, Whitford runs a pretty tight ship. He's in his mid forties and he has worked with Addison on several of his better-than-break-even action films. Sure, it would have been a real ego trip to have either Scorsese or Affleck as the director, but for all I know, Addison's references to them was a bunch of hooey, thrown out there in order to impress us and get us onboard.

A lot of the crew are made up of locals, but the core group—assistant directors, second- and third-unit directors, the cinematographer, the key grip, the property master and Leda, our set dresser, not to mention Emma's boss, Gerard Pruitt, who is head of the make-up department—have worked with Addison on several of his films, and have a non-spoken shorthand that keeps things moving between takes.

The tardiness of the picture's star has had them all on pins and needles.

Whomever she is, Film Donna has got to be a very big star! Otherwise, why would everyone be this nervous?

And from what Whitford just said, she'll be here any minute.

Oh my God, I can't meet her like this—in a yellow polka-dotted sundress and sandals. The dress is one of my favorites, but still—I need to change!

I turn to head back to our cabana when I see Jack trotting my way. "Hey, guess what? Abu has located Serena La Costa. She's on the mainland, in Caracas, and she's at least willing to talk to us. Abu's coming to get us, in a speedboat. Once we're in town, we'll have a car to get around. He'll be here any minute, so we better get cracking."

"Super! But"—I hesitate, because I know how this will sound: star struck. I take a deep breath and, as nonchalantly as I can, I say—"Whitford just got word that the movie's Donna will be here any minute. Can we hang around to see who she is?"

Whenever Jack is exasperated, he runs a hand through his hair. I've never seen it get stuck in his nice thick dark locks—until now. "You're kidding me, right? Serena's testimony gets us off the Most Wanted list, and you're more concerned about who plays you in this silly movie?"

"You're just being cruel, Jack. You heard Sebastian—it's brilliant!"

"Ah, well there you go! The writer of the damn thing says so himself." He folds his arms against his chest in protest. "And, as both his subject and his supplicant, you agree with him, I presume?"

His remarks are totally uncalled for. I'm just about to tell him where he can stick his sarcasm when an arm goes around my waist.

Sebastian's.

From the wince on his face, I know he heard what Jack called me. "I say, old boy, it's not every day one sees one's life made into a movie. Surely whatever caper you have in mind for—how did you put it? Oh yes, 'my subject and my supplicant'—can wait until the fake Mrs. Smith has the honor of meeting the woman she'll bring to life on the screen."

It's Jack's turn to frown. He doesn't like another man coming to my defense. A girl is supposed to have just one knight in shining armor.

When he sees I'm not budging from my stance, let alone out from under Sebastian's arm, he bows slightly and mutters, "Theory proven and point taken. Come find me when you're through paying homage to yourself, so we can get on with our real lives." He walks off.

"Cheeky bastard," Sebastian murmurs.

"No, he's right. It's truly silly of me to be this…this…silly over something so…well, silly." He's got me flustered. We supplicants get that way. To shake it off, I murmur, "You'll have to excuse me. I was headed back to our cabana."

He smiles. "Not to change into something else, I hope. You look ravishing as is."

"Oh! Well, that's kind of you to say." I'm still red from all the sun we're getting, so perhaps he can't see me blush.

"Donna, I meant what I said to Jack. You've done her—and me, for that matter—the honor of bringing you to life on the big screen. Take a few moments to savor it, even if Jack won't."

"He's not used to all this attention. For that matter, I'm not either." I sigh. "I don't know how you do it."

He chuckles. "Celebrity has its perks. In my regard, I get to hone my craft, to travel, and to meet those whose lives are a bit more interesting than my own. Right now, I'm living vicariously through you."

It's my turn to laugh. "Then I guess I'll have to make it as exciting as possible for you."

His eyes sweep over me. "Thus far, you're living up to all my expectations."

I don't know how to answer him. The whirring sound coming from overhead—a helicopter, from what we can see —saves me from having to do so.

"Ah, she's finally here! Shall we join the welcoming party?"

He holds out his hand.

Of course I take it. I don't have time to change, after all— but so what? Sebastian is right, she won't even notice.

She'll just be happy to meet me.

I know I'll feel the same way.

We reach the helicopter just as it starts its descent dead center onto the circular green in the center of the resort's driveway.

We're not the only ones there to greet it. The cast and crew are streaming out of the plantation house like the Munchkins, running to meet Glinda, in *The Wizard of Oz.*

She was the good witch, so I'll take that as a hopeful sign of things to come.

The chopper lands, but it's hard to see through its tinted glass windows. Finally, the engine is cut and the blades still to a lazy turn.

The door lifts up, and the pilot extends the air stair.

The first to clamber down is the reporter from *Variety*.

Finally, the long legs of our star, clad in five-inch Christian Dior over-the-knee stiletto boots.

Boots…on a beach?

I'm so fixated on her fashion faux pas that it takes a moment before her face registers with me—

Willow Higginbotham.

Really? The she-devil?

She's not alone. A harried woman is practically falling out of the helicopter beneath the weight of a six-piece matching set of Louis Vuitton luggage. Considering that the poor thing is wearing chinos from last decade and a turtleneck from the last millennium, I'm guessing the luggage isn't hers.

Behind her is a very thin man—also in thigh-high boots, and wearing even more makeup than Willow. He too carries luggage, but just one piece: a retro choo-choo case.

The last person to step out is another very thin man. He could be the first one's twin, down to the boots and the choo-choo. I guess Willow scored a matching set of acolytes as her posse.

Since I'm anything but, I storm back into the plantation house, and directly into Addison's suite of offices—

Where Addison is dictating an email—

To my son, who is tapping it out on his iPad.

"—on the studio lot. Please note that I did not agree to any terms which some sorry son-of-a-bitch pissant third-rate actor deems necessary—"

"Excuse me?" I shout.

All eyes turn my way.

"Yes, Mrs. Smith, is there something I can do for you?" Addison rolls his eyes—in front of my son, no less.

"I'll say"—I take a deep breath—"but not in front of my son."

Addison gives Jeff the high sign. "Scram, kid."

Jeff frowns as he passes me on his way out the door.

"Now, what can I do for you?" Addison's congenial tone could lull a baby into a happy stupor.

I am not a baby. Neither am I stupid. It's time I made that clear to him. "First off, you will not use expletives in front of my son!"

"Wait…" Addison shakes his head in awe. "That kid…he's yours?"

"Who the heck did you think he was?"

"I don't know just another of my revolving-door interns." He picks up the cup on the table beside him. "Wow. I'm impressed. The kid makes a mean cappuccino." He motions toward it. "Would you like one?"

"Frankly…yes." Jeff made that? Why hasn't he made one for me before now? *Grrrrr.* "I mean, no! I've got a bone to pick with you."

"Yeah, yeah, I know. Look, everyone in this business starts out as an unpaid intern. But hey, since it's your kid, I guess I can swing at least minimum wage for him."

"No, that's not why I'm...I mean, yes, of course Jeff should get paid for being your lackey!" All of a sudden, I miss the surf, and the sand and the sun. But no, this is why I get paid the big bucks—to knock heads. "What I mean to say is that I'm here because I don't approve of Willow Higginbotham as the actress to play Donna."

"Oh?" Addison takes a loud slurp of his cappuccino, then licks the foam mustache from his upper lip.

Classy.

"Sorry, but she just won't do," I insist. "Granted, she's a pretty woman, but let's face it—she can't act her way out of a paper bag. Not only that, she doesn't have the chops to pull off the gravitas and pathos of a thriller with this depth."

"I see." Addison nods sagely.

"Good! Then we're in agreement that she goes."

"Sorry, no can do." He looks at his watch.

I'm oblivious to broad hints. It's time he learned this first hand. "She goes, or we shut down production."

"Nowhere in the contract that you signed are you given approval of the actress to play you on the screen."

Ah, hell, he's got me there.

"How can you compare her to Amy Adams, or Jennifer Garner, or Jennifer Lawrence—let alone to me? She's the furthest thing from me!"

"You're right. You're a hard act to follow." He'd be easier to believe if he weren't yawning when he says it. "But Jeff thinks she'll grow into the role—"

"Who? You mean my son, the intern? Since when do you listen to a damn intern?"

"What can I say? He's got his finger on the pulse of the twelve-to-twenty-nine-year-old males who like movies where things go bang and boom." Addison wags his finger at me. "By the way, I thought we were doing away with the expletives."

"You're right, we are." A mother sets the example for others to follow. Addison, that asshole, is the perfect case in point.

"Listen, 'Mrs. Smith,' let's be honest with each other, okay? You're getting paid a pretty penny to put up and shut up. So, go lay on the beach. Or take in some target practice. In other words, do whatever it is you paid assassins do to unwind, okay? Now, would you like a cappuccino?" As he stands up, he pretends to brush imaginary lint off his producer's standard-issue black tee-shirt. In truth, it's a broad hint for me to get out of his face.

Even my son knows it, because as I stalk out of the room, he ducks his head in shame.

"Really, Jeff? You think that—inflated Barbie doll can play me in this movie?"

Jeff's head pops up. He squints as he contemplates the best way to answer the woman who gave birth to him after nine months of a pregnancy that straddled the hottest summer in California history, followed by a sixteen-hour natural labor. The best he can come up with is, "Granted, she's bigger on top, but I thought women like it when men think they're young and pretty." He shrugs. "Besides, she's not really supposed to be you. She's Jane Smith, the spy."

I guess for an eleven-year-old on the cusp of puberty, this is what passes for a compliment.

He's right about that. At my stage of life, I take them no matter how small. It's the thought that counts.

Still, I have to ask, "When the heck did you learn how to make a cappuccino?"

"Mom, if you're going to survive in this business, you have to pull out all the stops," he says mournfully.

He's right.

Okay, time for me to lead by example, to take control.

Maybe if I take Willow under my wing, she'll grow into the part, exceed my minimal expectations—

And earn that Oscar the role certainly deserves.

She came here a B-film rom-com queen, but she'll leave here a star. I'll see to that.

9

Reality Bites

"Sex is the quickest way to ruin a friendship."

Janeane Garofalo, as "Vickie"

IS THAT REALLY HER—YOU KNOW, YOUR FAVORITE ACTRESS? OH my God—yes! Since it's just the two of you in the ladies' room, she's now your captive audience. Your goal: to be just as captivating to her as you find her onscreen. With that in mind, here are a couple of things you never say to a celebrity when you see them for the very first time:

- *Wrong Sentence #1: "Hmmm. For some reason, you look much younger onscreen." Yeah, duh, that's because she has an army of hair and make-up people who work on her for hours fussing and gussying every inch of her face, body and hair. She doesn't need a perfect stranger to remind her that she's less than perfect.*

- *Wrong Sentence #2: "Hmmm. For some reason, you look a lot thinner onscreen." You would, too, if you wore three sets of Spanx under every outfit, and the few extra pounds on your thighs were removed, thanks to digital movie magic.*

Sadly, in real life, what you see is what you get.
You know this, just by looking in the mirror.
I guess that's why you'd shoot anyone who has the nerve to say these sentences to you, too.

WHEN I GET TO THE SET, I FIND JACK IS THERE, TOO. HE MUST have the very same idea about encouraging Willow to bring her A game because he's chatting her up.

Yeah! He likes her! He really, really likes her!

From what I can tell, he's turning on the charm he's so famous for: the deep laugh, the naughty grin, that way in which he leans in close, as if he's known you all his life.

No woman leans away.

Take Willow, for example, not only does she lean in, she reaches up—

And pulls him down, into a lip lock.

Um…no.

I tap her on the back. "Miss Higginbotham?"

Jack's eyes open wide when he sees me. He tries to shake his head, as if to tell me what I can see with my own eyes: *It's all her fault.*

On the other hand, Willow must be lost in thought because she doesn't even bother to turn around.

I clear my throat loudly. "Miss Higginbotham, I'm honored to finally meet you!"

She straightens up. Despite the amount of Botox in her forehead that may be masking any frown, her posture says it all: *I am not happy.*

The cast and crew gasps. Apparently, they're impressed with my gravitas, too.

Good, I've broken the spell Jack has over her—

But when she turns to face me, she's glaring. "Whitford! Who is this person? Have you forgotten that it says in my contract that no one is to make eye contact with me? Fire her…immediately!"

Whitford is turning fifty shades of gray. "But—but Willow, this is the woman whose life you're portraying. This is *Jane Smith*."

Slowly she turns back toward me. When she does, her stony frown has been transformed into a cherubic pout. "Oh! Mrs. Smith, I'm so sorry!" She takes both my hands in hers. "Do forgive me! You would not believe how, at times, I become overwhelmed by fans."

There, that's better. An olive branch has been extended. I'm gracious enough to forgive and forget. "I can see where a lot of autograph requests would get tedious after a while."

"Well, yes. But that's not what I meant." Her chuckle floats on the air like a feather in a summer breeze. "It's just that I had no idea that 'Jane' is…well, middle-aged." She thinks for a moment. "I envisioned you—her—much younger. You know, my age."

I've read profiles on Willow in *Vanity Fair* and *People*. At the most, she's a few months, not a few years, younger than me.

If Jack thinks his coughing fit will divert me from the task of testing the brittleness of her not-so-much-younger bones by pummeling her within an inch of her not-so-much-younger life, it's not working. But before I can throw my punch, Sebastian guides Willow just beyond the range of my fist, and toward the plantation house. "Let me introduce myself—Sebastian Gillingham, your screenwriter and humble servant." He takes her small-boned hand in his in order to bow over it, grazing it with his lips. "Alas, as much as I'm sure you and Mrs. Smith would enjoy getting to know each other, duty calls. I'd be honored to answer any questions you have regarding the script and my own thoughts on your character's sensitivity, which no doubt will grow under your gentle touch."

Willow responds by licking her lips, leaving him no doubt that something sensitive will be growing under her touch.

I presume it won't be her character.

This is confirmed as Willow purses her Collagen-inflated lips into a pout and opines, "I've been such a bad girl, Mr. Gillingham! You see, somehow I've lost my script."

"Yes, that was a very naughty thing to do! A severe dressing-down is in order, to be sure." His admonishment is more of an alluring promise than any serious threat. "Alas, not today. Your writer and your director await with bated breath your insightful interpretation of your character in her very first scenes, and they'll accommodate you in any way they can."

It must be the response she'd hoped for because she rewards him with a dazzling smile. "Will I be able to read it off of cue cards?"

Whitford slaps his forehead with his hand and motions for a production assistant to get right on it. Seeing him on the move, everyone else is, too.

Including me. In three strides, Jack is at my side. "I take it you're ready to hit the mainland now?"

"The sooner, the better." I'm too ashamed to look him in the eye. If I was ever Sebastian's sycophant, I'm not anymore.

I understand why he feels the need to fawn over Willow. She is, after all, the real star of this picture.

At the same time, I don't have to respect him for groveling to her whims.

By now, Jack and I are practically running to the pier where we're to rendezvous with Abu.

Time to hit the mainland for a much-needed reality check.

IN THE STREETS OF CARACAS, WE DUCK AND DODGE TO AVOID two roving armies: the National Guard and paramilitary troops known as *colectivos*—both of whom support the current regime.

Serena's home is located in the Altamira district in the *Chacao* municipality of Caracas. Its numerous hotels, restaurants and shopping malls flank Plaza Francia, a beautiful communal park. This upscale upper- and middle-class neighborhood is—or I should say, was—considered a safe haven in this large turbulent and often dangerous city, until the latest round of civil unrest.

After driving into the city, Abu pulls up to a repair shop within a few blocks of the plaza. "We'll have to walk from here. I've mapped out a route I hope is safe, but there are no guarantees," he warns us. "If we run into any *colectivos* or *motorizados*—those are thugs who do drive-by shootings—keep your heads down. They think nothing of beating, shooting or jailing anyone who looks at them cross-eyed, including the international journalists who are here to cover the uprising. If we get separated, we'll rendezvous back here at the garage."

No wonder Addison got the resort location for a pittance.

"How can anyone live like this?" I mutter.

"The middle class has been asking themselves that for the past year," Abu explains. "The country's university students have rallied them to speak out for real elections, in light of what the last two regimes have done to the country: crumbling infrastructure, an inflation rate of almost sixty percent, and a crime and murder rate that is the highest in the world. But the money flowing in from Venezuela's oil wells will eventually drown them out. Serena's husband, Tomas Marianni, teaches computer science at Colegio San Ignacio de Loyola. He allows the students to use his classroom to access the computers for social networking in support of the protests."

A few blocks later, we come across the campus of the

college. National Guardsmen stand on every corner, rifles at the ready. Abu disappears into a shadow. The soldiers stare at Jack and me as we pass. At first, I'm surprised when Jack kisses me deeply in front of one. Then I remember the movie theater—where we saw *She's So Hot* and I recognize the method to his madness. To play along, I giggle and scold Jack by saying "No, no! *Vamanos!*"

The soldier smirks at our mild flirtations. We're just some silly couple in love.

By now, Abu has slipped past the guards and is a block ahead of us, and on the other side of the street. He walks into the entryway of a small apartment building. Unlike many of the others surrounding it, this one is only three stories high. Each of the apartments has a deck of some sort.

When we get to the front door, Abu has already picked the lock and murmurs, "Second floor, southwest corner. It's apartment two-zero-two. Knock twice, then twice again. I'll stay out here and keep watch."

We nod and head up the stairs.

We quickly find the apartment. When we give the coded knock, the door opens slightly. Serena's face stares out at us. She looks a little plumper. She also looks anxious as she beckons us out of the hall.

We shake her hand. Her husband, Tomas, is a short, slim man with an unruly mop of dark brown hair, and a bushy mustache. He stands against the wall. He holds an infant boy in his arms.

The child explains Serena's plumpness. "Congratulations," I say.

Finally, she smiles. "Thank you, Mrs. Stone. As you can

see, I am a mother myself, finally." She takes her husband's arm. "It is an honor to introduce you to my husband, Tomas Marianni, and my son, Paulo."

Jack and I shake his hand. I reach out for the baby. Tomas waits for Serena's nod of approval before allowing me to take him.

Still, Tomas does not smile. "My wife has told me about her captivity at the hands of this terrible man, Jonah Breck. I am grateful that you saved her from a tragic fate. We will forever be in your debt," he says warily. "I take it your visit is not social. This is not a great time to be in Venezuela for its citizens, let alone Americanos. These days, everyone watches everyone else. Do you know if you were followed here?"

"We did our best to avoid surveillance," I assure him. "Serena owes us nothing. Breck was scum, and got what he deserved. However, the man who killed him, my ex-husband, is now one of the most powerful men in our country. He has doctored the webcam footage that was taken that day to make it look as if I was the one who killed Breck and Antoinette. Only Serena's eye-witness testimony can save me from jail and possible execution."

Serena's eyes fog over with fear. "I—I had hoped to put those memories behind me forever. Testifying is the right thing to do, but...I cannot leave my infant son or my husband."

Jack puts his hand on her shoulder. "We can arrange to have them accompany you." He hesitates, then adds, "With all the turmoil going on here, if both of you would prefer to emigrate to the United States, we will do what we can to help you with that as well."

Serena and Tomas turn to each other. Their faces reflect a flood of emotions. Surprise gives way to elation. Hope is tempered with fear. Almost simultaneously, both faces glow with a sense of determination.

"As much as we love our country, our friends and our families, we now have Paulo to consider. I will go, as long as my family is by my side."

I hug her fervently. "Thank you, Serena, for giving me back my freedom."

"It is the least I could do for the woman who saved my life," she whispers in my ear.

"Our associate, Abu, will make the necessary arrangements," Jack explains. "You'll be contacted in a couple of weeks as to where to go, and who to meet. In the meantime, don't mention these plans to anyone, even those you love most, or believe you can trust. Your lives depend on it."

They nod in unison. Their looks of determination do not leave their faces as Jack and I slip out the door.

The lights in the building's lobby are off. Abu rises from one of the shadows. When he gives us the high sign, we slip out a side entrance, and trace our path back to the street where we left our car.

On the way back to the speedboat, Jack and Abu discuss the logistics of getting Serena and her family out of the country. I'm silent until Isla Margarita comes into view.

It's twilight. The sun is setting into the shimmering blue tropical waters. Abu slows the boat so that its engine's growl is barely a purr.

Jack comes up behind me and whispers in my ear, "A penny for your thoughts."

"You'll have to come up with much more money than that," I warn him. "At this very moment, my thoughts are priceless. I've been envisioning the day we'll be free to enter the US, and Carl can't do anything to hurt us, ever again."

"Thanks to Serena, that day is closer than you think." He nuzzles my ear. "In the meantime, there is still a lot to be done. Whitford insists all scenes for the Hilldale interior shots will be done within the next three days. The production then moves on to its next location, Paris, where we'll meet with the asset—the man who worked as Carl's handler when he was merely a hitman for the Quorum. He can document Carl's bloody rise to the top. Then onto England, where apparently Dominic has convinced a witness to testify on record regarding Carl and one of his hits. Soon, we'll be free to go home, Donna."

Home, to Hilldale.

I can't wait.

Until then, we'll have a few more days in the sun.

And then back to work, proving our innocence and Carl's treachery.

It's why we get paid the big bucks.

10

Some Like It Hot

"So you got pinched in the elevator, so what? Would you rather be picking lead out of your navel?"

Tony Curtis, as "Joe/Josephine"

AS THE NEWLY ELECTED PRESIDENT OF YOUR FAVORITE STAR'S FAN club, you can now set the protocol, which club members must follow! Here are a few set-in-stone rules:

Any communication with the assistant to the personal assistant to the star in question should come from you, no ifs, ands or buts. By being the mouthpiece of all fawning acolytes, you'll prove yourself irreplaceable —

--Unlike the assistant to the personal assistant. Any screw-up on her part allows you to backchannel the fans' discontent directly to the personal assistant, which will eventually get her underling fired.

And guess what? You're now up for the position!

In this position, you'll prove your mettle! Feel free to audio record the personal assistant's grouses about the star's incessant requests. Now that you have access to the private cell phone digits of The One You Adore Above All Others, you can text her the audio feed.

Voilà, *as soon as the personal assistant is fired, you're now in the number one position!*

As such, you know better than to hire the gal who replaced you as fan club president. Instead, you go for the time-honored tradition of hiring deaf and dumb eunuchs to fill out your star's posse. The star you adore will appreciate your resourcefulness for keeping gossipmongers at bay, perhaps to the point of offering you a job for life—

Something you've always wanted.

One more word of advice: Be careful what you wish for…

ACCORDING TO THE TABLOIDS, WILLOW'S MATING SEASON RUNS concurrent to her filming schedule. From what I've seen over the past week, I can vouch for this.

Leda the wardrobe mistress's prediction that sparks would fly between Reed and Willow was spot on. Apparently, their sex scenes are practically porn.

Or as Addison puts it, "To hell with a 'director's cut.' There's going to be a 'producer's cut,' and it's going to be triple-X rated! The investors will recoup their money in no time!"

The stars' friskiness doesn't end when the cameras quit rolling. The moans emanating from Willow's cabana are so loud and so continuous that the Isla Margarita's wild parrots have abandoned its banyan trees, likely never to be seen again.

To Whitford's relief, Willow and Reed's foreplay and post-coital coziness include running lines together. "If they could memorize their parts while actually screwing, we could cut the production schedule in half," he crows.

"Have someone read it to them," Addison suggests. "You know, like a fluffer."

Unfortunately, Reed has a short attention span. I find this out the hard way. I'm passing Reed's bungalow just as Candy Cunningham, Willow's stunt double, is departing. Thank goodness she's too busy buttoning her blouse to see me. I duck out of sight just in time.

Here's hoping that jerk, Reed, can keep his other dalliances on the QT until the production wraps.

I realize the odds of that are slim to none when I'm summoned to Willow's cabana. It seems that every other woman working on the movie is here, too. Whitford is also present, as are the thin twins who are charged with keeping Willow ravishing, both onscreen and off. The twins have sly smiles, but Whitford is not smiling.

Seeing that we're all gathered, Willow's female assistant, Augusta, locks the door behind us.

I push my way toward Emma until we're side by side. Like the rest of the women, she looks anxious. "Do you know what this is all about?" I ask her.

"Yes! I heard Willow's Pretty Posse gossiping about it in the make-up trailer," she whispers, nodding toward the thin twins. In fact, sometimes I wonder if she keeps these know-it-alls under her bed when she's entertaining Reed. They're certainly slight enough to fit under it. "Apparently, Augusta saw some woman come out of Reed's cabana. She went in snooping and found a thong—and it wasn't Willow's! Now Willow is on the war path!" A tear rolls down her cheek.

Oh, no.

I grasp Emma's hand. "Oh…Emma!"

"Yes, I know, it was so stupid of me! It happened almost a week ago now. Afterward, he forgot about it, as if it never even happened!" she bows her head, ashamed. "Just yesterday he tried to pick me up again. He didn't even remember my name, let alone that he and I have already…you know."

Unfortunately, I do. "How about Arnie? Does he know?"

She frowns. "He saw me leaving Reed's cabana. He won't even look at me now." Tears fill her eyes again.

"*Shhhhh!*" Augusta hisses at the murmuring crowd. "Willow must speak!"

The crowd freezes.

Willow makes her grand entrance from the cabana's bedroom. She holds a tiny purse in her hand. She takes her place in the center of the group, which lines every inch of the cabana's grand living room.

"It has come to my attention that someone is sleeping with my leading man, Reed Horwitch." With a flourish, Willow opens the bag—

And pulls out a black thong.

Everyone gasps.

"Well, my little pretty, you left the wrong calling card. It has been your undoing. Your confession will now be public.

Punishment will be anything but merciful—a one-way ticket off our little paradise, and the disgrace of being blacklisted from any future Montague production, let alone a film starring me."

Her ridiculous behavior is tempting me to admit to the act, but I can't stand the thought that anyone would presume I'd go anywhere near creepy Reed, so I keep my mouth shut.

Holding the thong high over her head, she circles the crowd slowly, like a panther sniffing out its cornered prey, all the while taking her time to scrutinize each and every face.

I find Candy in the crowd. She has a smirk on her face. She's been Willow's stuntwoman on other jobs, and will never jeopardize her income. If Candy keeps her mouth shut, she's got a job for as long as Willow's face holds out. Apparently, the star needs a double on every movie involving vertical exertion, even if it's just bending down to tie her shoes.

"No takers, eh?" Willow's words curdle with contempt. "Well then, you better hope I like your face. If I don't, you're out of here anyway—one by one, until the bad girl amongst you confesses."

The women are fidgeting like crazy now. With each step Willow takes closer to Emma and me, the more color drains from Emma's face. Her hand is clammy. Suddenly I feel it rising—

But I hold it firmly in mine.

I won't let her take the fall. We need her on this mission.

She shakes her head furiously. "I can't let someone lose

her job because of what I did," she whispers. She starts to speak out again, but I slap my hand over her mouth—

"It's mine!" Leda, the wardrobe mistress, yells out.

At least, I think it's Leda who screamed. Quite frankly, so many women are speaking at once that it could have been any of them.

Everyone scrutinizes everyone else as, in unison, they exclaim, "What? You too?"

Well, what do you know?

The pandemonium is not helped in the least by Willow shouting, "Alright then, you're all fired!"

Emma is so upset that she runs out of the room.

The rest of us are on her tail.

As I pass Whitford, I hear him warn Willow, "No, sorry, but I can't fire all of them! It would mean shutting down the production. Addison can't afford that—and neither can you, Willow. Let's just all put this behind us—oh! Sorry, wrong way to put it, I guess."

Willow storms off to the bedroom.

She's wailing again.

The birds are gone for good by now. I guess the rest of the island's inhabitants would leave as well, if they could fly.

FOR WILLOW, THE REALIZATION THAT REED WAS BOINKING HALF the crew, means all out war.

"To retaliate, she's bedding Reed's stuntman, Ellis," Emma tells me.

Talk about bad karma. Ellis is also Candy's husband.

Should either Candy or Ellis find out about the others' dalliances, they would likely walk off the picture, and the production would shut down anyway.

In the meantime, Willow has added fuel to the fire with a Tweet making a comparison of her lovers' sexual prowess:

@WillowHigginbotham

@ReedHorwitch has stunted growth where it counts most, but @ReedHorwitch's stuntman: is THE MAN!

A half hour later, Reed's fans—who call themselves Reed's WhoreBitches—launch a Twitter hate campaign against Willow:

@ReedsWhoreBitches

@WillowHigginbotham is gaining so much weight on @WifeyAssassin that she should change her name to @PillowBigOnBottom!

A photo of Willow is attached to the post. It has been doctored to make her look three times wider than her natural (okay, make that surgically-enhanced) physique.

To add insult to injury, so many WhoreBitches have retweeted the post that it's taken even less time than Ellen DeGeneres' Academy Award tweet to crash Twitter.

Publicly humiliated, Candy has requested a separate cabana from her husband. Knowing his temper, she keeps mum about her own indiscretions.

It's now all-out war between Willow and Reed. They've

both requested that all mutual scenes be shot separately, using the others' double as a stand-in.

Whitford refuses to do it.

To retaliate, they fluster each other by muttering cruel asides.

Production is almost at a standstill. In the meantime, Jack and I are climbing the walls. Every day we spend on Isla Margarita puts us one day further away from proving our innocence.

"Maybe I should go on ahead," Jack suggests. "You and the kids can catch up with me there."

I shake my head emphatically. "No way! That would mean flying commercial—not exactly a smart thing to do when you're sitting on top of the Interpol's Wanted Persons list! If you remember, one of the reasons we agreed to work with Addison is because of Montague Studios' private plane. It's our free ride to France, and then England afterward."

"What good does it do any of us if the plane is sitting on the tarmac?" He's pacing again. "We've got to come up with a Plan B."

"My Plan B is to murder the two idiots playing us," I grumble.

"I get the feeling their stunt doubles feel the same way," Jack says. "Emma tells me Ellis and Candy had a big fight the other night."

Arnie knocks on our door. "Hey, can I speak to you both? I've…I've got a bit of a problem."

I'll say. I don't know what I can say to help Emma get a reprieve, but I'll do my best. I give him a really big smile. "What's up?"

"I think I'm in trouble. I was rigging two explosives for the second unit's next scene—a car chase—when I got a call from some guy claiming to be Whitford's assistant. He told me to report to the main soundstage. When I got there, Whitford said he never called. A moment later, I get a call from a woman requesting that I meet with Addison. When I got to his office, Jeff was there. He said the producer never made a call—that Addison had been in meetings with the stars all morning, reading them the riot act. When I went back to the Special Effects shed, the explosive devices were gone." He frowns. "What should I do now? If I tell the second unit director, I'll probably get fired."

"Not if I can help it," Jack assures him. "Go back to the shed and rig up two replacement devices. In the meantime, Donna and I will see if we can find them, and more importantly, who took them."

Arnie nods furtively. "They're wrapped in red tape. Each is the size of a paperback book. Thanks!" With shoulders slumped, he's out the door.

Jack grabs his cell. "While I search the cabanas and exterior sets, you take the plantation house. Corner anyone looking suspicious, even if the devices aren't in sight."

"Will do," I say. My kiss expresses the thought uppermost in my mind: *stay safe, because I can't afford to lose you.*

THE INCENDIARY DEVICES ARE NOWHERE TO BE FOUND.

Whoever has them has hidden them well.

Arnie must have handed off the replacement devices

because the second unit has already set up for the car chase scene. In it, "John" and "Jane"—or in this case, Ellis and Candy—are in separate cars, chasing down a bad guy in a third car. They will come at him from different directions, shooting at him simultaneously.

Of course, one of the bullets "kills" him. When this happens, the car will roll and explode, using Arnie's replacement devices.

The scene is being shot on the empty private jet way adjacent to the resort. I watch as Candy and Ellis take off on the same road, in different directions. Through my ear bud, I hear Chad, the second unit director, shouting instructions to them. When they are far enough apart, he commands them to turn the cars around so that they face each other. They then wait for the signal that will put them in motion.

The bad guy's car takes off when its driver hears, "Action!" It approaches them from a lane that intersects their road.

Candy and Ellis finally get their signal and they're rolling toward each other. The cars—one is a Porsche, and the other is a Ferrari—take just a few seconds to accelerate past sixty miles an hour—

Only to explode—simultaneously.

"What the Hell?" Chad screams. "Cut! Cut! Oh my God!"

The fire unit comes running. They hose down the infernos with fire-retardant foam so that the med techs can pull Ellis and Candy from the wreckage.

The production's medical emergency team has split up into two groups, one for each of the victims. I watch them work furiously to save the couple's lives.

After whispering something to one of the responders, Ellis succumbs.

Candy dies a few minutes later.

Jack, Arnie and I watch as the med techs cover their bodies before hoisting them onto gurneys and wheeling them away.

The lead emergency responder heads over to Chad. We walk over just in time to hear Chad exclaim, "What do you mean, they made 'final confessions?'"

"I'm not kidding," the team leader swears. "Ellis said, 'If she lives, tell her I rigged her car. If she doesn't, I'll see her in hell.' At the same time, Candy was telling her team almost exactly the same thing."

At least now we know who took the IADs.

Chad is too shaken to say anything.

He walks toward the plantation house to break the news to Whitford.

AN HOUR LATER, ADDISON GATHERS THE CAST AND CREW together.

He's so longwinded that I find myself tuning him out. At the same time, I hold my breath as I wait for him to say what I fear is the inevitable:

The production is being shuttered.

Since the family Stone can't go back to the US, we'll have to figure out some other way to get off this island.

Or else go back to the mainland and join Venezuela's revolution.

"—and so, in memory of our fallen colleagues, let's rally as a team and as a family! Let's show the world their lives weren't taken in vain! This movie will be dedicated to the memories of…"—he pauses. Jeff stands on tiptoe, to whisper their names in his ear—"of Candy and Ellis Cunningham."

The show must go on—at least for Montague Studios' stockholders.

Love hurts, but jealousy kills.

I didn't need Candy and Ellis to teach me this lesson when I've got Carl breathing down my back.

11

American Psycho

"My need to engage in homicidal behavior on a massive scale cannot be corrected, but I have no other way to fulfill my needs."

Christian Bale, as "Patrick Bateman"

EVEN IF YOU CAN'T WALK DOWN THE RED CARPET FOR A premiere, you're quite welcome to stand on the sidelines and cheer the film's stars as they make their grand entrances. However, you're wise to follow these do's and don'ts:

Do stay behind the red velvet rope. If you're caught on the carpet, you'll be goose-stepped off the property by two gorillas in tuxedoes. Take this as a hint that you're not getting anywhere near that carpet, let alone those who tread it so regally.

Don't reach over the rope and grab a star. You are not at a petting zoo, despite the aforementioned tuxedoed gorillas who now have their paws wrapped firmly around you.

Do leave all sidearms at home. Despite your desire to give your favorite star a snappy military salute, the embarrassment of being arrested as a possible terrorist won't encourage him to appreciate you, let alone get you any closer than five hundred yards of his next public appearance.

Don't try to crash the carpet by getting primped up and hiring a limo to drop you off. The guest list to these things is always written in blood—that of the publicist in charge of the event. They are orchestrated to perfection, so no matter how dazzling your over-the-shoulder smolder, she'll think nothing of wrestling you to the ground herself, so that the real stars can arrive on time.

THE DEATHS OF THEIR STUNT DOUBLES LEFT THE STARS OF OUR picture duly chastened. Replacements were on the set the very next day. However, both are so plug ugly that even Willow and Reed wince when they see them.

Smart move on Addison's part, or perhaps Jeff's.

Three weeks ago, shooting shifted to Paris. The production is moving through its list of tourist-friendly outdoor location shoots. In the movie, they will be sinister, as well as beautiful and familiar.

Whitford is shooting some choice, universally recognizable interiors, too. These include a salon in the Louvre; the pews in Notre Dame; Printemps Department Store; and a suite at the Georges V, the grand hotel where the leads, the director, the producer and the family Stone (greatly pleased) have been placed.

The supposed-child actors are needed at some of these locations, but most of the filming revolves around the leads.

To be honest, I'd kill for the heroine's wardrobe. Willow has it written into her contract that she gets to keep any dress she likes.

She's lucky she's not my size.

Mary and Rachel are still joined at the hip. Having been to Paris for a couple of film shoots already, Rachel is an accommodating tour guide. When they come back from their many romps, they sequester themselves, sometimes for hours on end. I catch the two of them whispering and giggling. When I ask them why, they freeze and make up some excuse so flimsy I can see right through it.

Trisha is now so comfortable with hotel living that Jack calls her "our little Eloise." She prowls every new home-away-from-home from top to bottom so that the floor plans and grounds become second nature to her. She orders room service like a pro, and charms the housekeeping staff into leaving extra chocolates on our pillows.

Willow and Reed's shenanigans put the production off schedule by a couple of weeks, and that has Jack and me worried. Abu sends Serena and Tomas coded messages via Twitter, reassuring them that their stateside trip will take place any day now—that is, when Jack and I can join them and keep them safe.

In the meantime, we make the most of our time here. For once, we get to enjoy playing the role of tourists, relaxing in the city's numerous parks and museums. We owe it to ourselves. Our last time here was much too eventful.

Quorum assassins chased us as we followed up on a clue to the terrorist group's next act of mass violence.

Aunt Phyllis has also found a way to keep busy during her hours away from the children. Her nightly poker games with the crew are adding some heft to her nest egg.

"If that Reed guy shows up, I'm switching the game to strip poker," she promises.

I don't have the heart to tell her he's not her type. She may already be aware of this, since he stays far away from the card players. He'd much prefer to play doctor. Now that we're off our intimate island, he's free to pick up anyone walking down the Champs-Élysées.

"His room needs its own revolving door," Jack mutters. "Every liaison is an affair to forget."

Sebastian's room is the opposite. No one is allowed either in or out of it, not even the hotel's housekeepers. He insists he needs peace and quiet to complete his scripts for the next season of *Bloomsbury*. To help him keep track of the show's many plot threads, he travels with a full set of scripts from previous season's episodes.

He grudgingly leaves his room when called to the set when, for whatever reason, a line needs to be tweaked. In that case, either Jack or I need to be there, too, since our contract calls for us to have dialogue approval as well.

As we stand on the sidelines listening to Willow and Reed butcher their lines, Sebastian assuages his disappointment by teasing me. "As always, you look ravishing, Mrs. Smith. I miss our little script assignations."

"I do, too," I say. "Here's a thought! Perhaps I can help you with *Bloomsbury*."

For some reason, he finds this laugh-out-loud funny.

"I'm offended at your response, Sebastian. I'm not a complete illiterate, you know."

"I have no desire to offend, madam." He bows his head in mock shame. "In truth, the joke is on me, not you. I can only imagine what nuances you'd instill in my heroines. With you putting words in their mouths, Virginia and Vanessa would become much better people indeed."

"Thank you for the compliment," I say sincerely. "But I don't think the critics—or more importantly, the viewing public—would agree with you. Mary, for one, is crazy about the show! Lately she's been watching it incessantly. I can see it popping up on our Netflix viewed list."

"Yes, so I've been told, by Mary. In fact, if you wouldn't mind asking her to cool her ardor for my attentions—platonic, let me assure you—I'd be forever in your debt."

"Has she been a bother?"

"I'm sure Rachel has put her up to it. They aren't exactly stalking me, but they corner me at every opportunity with a list of questions about the show's characters and plots." He sighs. "Maybe I can convince JK Rowling to release another *Harry Potter* book, so they can find another target for their literary devotion."

"I'll ask her not to disturb you any further."

"It would be greatly appreciated…Ah, Jack—excuse me, I mean 'John,' seems to be waving you over. Are you two off again on some urban adventure?" He straightens the collar of my jacket, a retro dusty rose number I picked up from a street vendor who insisted it was vintage Chanel. It may not be, but in any event, it meets my two prerequisites: it's pretty and it keeps me warm.

"Sorry, no secret missions. Just some sightseeing." I glance over in the direction of his gaze.

Of course I'm lying to Sebastian. Abu must have made the connection with Carl's former handler. Jack's subtle wink is a high sign for us to get moving.

We're about to meet the man who inspired Carl to join the Quorum—and lived to tell about it.

ERIC WEBER LIVES ALMOST TWO HOURS OUTSIDE OF PARIS, IN A small French village called Dormans, located in the Marne Region.

Once outside of Paris proper, we find ourselves on small roads taking us over rolling hills, lush with vines that will soon be budding with the white grapes from which the region's renowned champagnes are created. The countryside is dotted with ancient churches and the ruins of centuries-old castles.

Eventually, we turn onto a narrow lane, bordered on both sides by high trees. Two hectares later, it dead-ends at the front gate of a grand estate, which is flanked by vineyards on all sides. The main house is a castle made of blocks of dark gray stone. Its rooftop turrets are ancient, but the men with guns standing sentry are not.

There are two other guards in a secure post at the entry gate. When Jack gives his name, they nod and allow us through.

We drive another half hectare to the formidable two story wood doors at the entry to the castle.

Jack and I park and get out of the car. As we walk toward the doors, they open outward soundlessly. The only thing I can hear is my heart beating in my chest.

What the hell have we gotten ourselves into?

The massive foyer has two staircases, one at each end, which lead to a mezzanine over the foyer. A man—perhaps in his early seventies—stands between the staircases. His broad shoulders are outlined in a suit that fits his body like a glove. Not a hair on his steel-gray mane is out of place. His military stance keeps his spine straight, his hands at his sides, and his eyes alert.

Yes, I can imagine this man would have inspired Carl.

To what ends, I can only guess.

He is quite aware of Jack's presence, but he only has eyes for me.

His voice is commanding without having to raise it above a murmur. "Ah! Finally, I meet Simon's wife! Or I presume you'd prefer I call you Mrs. Stone?"

The accent is German.

I have never forgotten that voice.

I've only heard it once before—when Carl was still my husband, and I so naively believed his position with Acme involved high finance, and that his far-flung trips involved the care and feeding of high-rolling international investors. After coming home from one such trip, he jumped into the shower, leaving his cell phone on top of the bed. I answered it when it rang, mistaking it for my phone.

This man was the caller, talking rapidly in his native

tongue. By the time he realized I was not whom he'd expected, Carl was out of the shower. He took the phone from me and closed it without a word to either me or the caller.

It was the first time I suspected my husband was keeping secrets from me.

"DO YOU DRINK CHAMPAGNE?" ERIC WEBER ASKS ME AS JACK and I stroll with him through his vineyard, which seems to go on for as far as the eye can see.

"I will, but I lean toward reds," I confess.

He smiles. "It was a fifty-fifty chance that you'd say no. I'm glad I'm not a betting man."

"Aren't you?" I raise my hand in order to shield my face from the high afternoon sun. "I mean, you took a very big chance on Carl, considering his position at Acme. And you're taking a very big chance now, in agreeing to testify against him."

Within the past hour, Eric has already told us what we want to hear—that he's willing to go stateside to be deposed about his role in turning Carl from an Acme assassin to a Quorum double agent; to turn over a list of Carl's hits, many involving agents and assets working for US intelligence agencies; and to provide documentation of Carl's initiatives in recruiting Quorum agents and assets throughout the world.

In return, Eric Weber gets worldwide immunity.

Eric shakes his head. "Carl never saw himself as a mere

assassin—or for that matter, a company man. The Quorum offered Carl something he could never have with Acme—actual power and real money. Granted, your agents are well paid, but not on the scale of the payday that comes with bringing a country to its knees." He smiles. "Then again, money is sterile. These days you don't even get the joy of rolling around in it. Instead, you move it from one electronic deposit account to another. What's the fun in that?" he shrugs. "In the Quorum, Carl had the added benefit of moving up the ladder. Granted, back in those days it was more like the *Hunger Games*. Quorum agents were pitted against each other—not only on kills, but on bigger missions, such as commanding a terrorist cell on its next mission, or blackmailing a country. Those who were successful lived to see another payday."

"Dog-eat-dog, just like Mary Kay distributors," I murmur.

He raises a brow. "I'll take your word for it. As for Carl, he proved to be the one dog smarter than his masters. After Breck's ignominious death at Carl's hand—or was it yours, my dear? With all the rumors flying around, I don't know whom to believe—he didn't know whom to trust. Thus, the massacre of those Quorum members in London, right under your noses."

"How did you happen to live to see another day"—Jack asks—"and in such sumptuous surroundings?"

"This is nothing more than a gilded cage." Eric points to the guards positioned on the roof. "If he could, Carl would have my head on a stake. Yes, I have something that keeps him at bay, but my hold over him is gossamer thin." His eyes shift from Jack to me. "You see, I know the whereabouts of the microdot, which holds the code to access the DaaS cloud with the Acme worldwide directory of agents and assets."

My heart leaps into my throat. So, Carl used it as a bargaining chip to stay alive.

Still, Jack and I have to pretend this bit of intel is still valuable. "You have it here?" I ask.

"It was left with someone very close to Carl." He smiles. "That is all I can say—for now. Should our joint effort to put Carl in prison be successful, I'll let you know who has it."

"Why would you do this?" Jack asks. "Why not get it yourself?"

"Power is a younger man's game, for those who wish to make their mark, or leave behind a legacy. I have no family and no heirs. I have all the money I will need for several lifetimes. Most of all, I have no need to destroy the world. I much prefer living in it, and enjoying it. With Carl out of the way, I'll do more of it." Eric beckons us on down the hill. "Come now, I'll show you my private cellar, where we will share a glass of my best champagne, and toast the downfall of my Simon, and your Carl."

———————————————

12

They Shoot Horses, Don't They?

———————————————

"I may not know a winner when I see one, but I sure as hell can spot a loser."

Gig Young, as "Rocky"

BEFORE YOU WIN YOUR ACADEMY AWARD FOR THE ROLE OF A lifetime, you must first be cast in a movie. (Yes, I know—a small detail; still I felt it wise to mention.) To that end, here are a few tips to help launch you into the firmament of stardom:

- *Tip #1: Don't just memorize the lines—embody the role! If you're to be a teen dream queen, look like a slut and eat enough pizza to get a few zits on your face. If you're to be a drug-addled prostitute, wear your roomie's whore couture, hire a pimp to attend your audition with you, and shoot up before you go in to read for the part. Even if the pimp ends up robbing everyone in the place, you'll certainly impress the casting director by the lengths you'll go to just to get the part.*

- *Tip #2: The fact that you didn't get a callback doesn't mean you should give up on the role. Go ahead and text the casting director to see if she lost your telephone number. Better yet, wait outside the front door of her house. By letting her know you know where she lives, even if the role goes to someone else, believe me, she'll never forget your face—and neither will the local police.*
- *Tip #3: If you don't get the role, be philosophical about it by remembering there are other ones out there better suited for your talents. You know, like the role of waiter. Or dog walker. Or as a personal assistant to the star whose life you covet. Just remember—the whole world is your stage!*

"AH! I LOVE THE SMELL OF FOX URINE IN THE MORNING!" Dominic Fleming inhales deeply. He has been tapped as a consultant for the day. With his nose still up in the air— granted, a permanent position for it—he scans the woods just beyond Castle Drogo, in Devon, England, where the film crew has set up for a fox hunt scene.

In it, the fox is not the hunters' true prey. Soon, all guns will be turned on our heroine and her hero. Thank goodness they're loaded with blanks.

To escape, they will gallop over hill, dale, and hedge. When the hero's horse is shot and the heroine's mare goes lame, they'll have to put it out if its misery before running for their lives.

But viewers need not worry. The movie will carry a disclaimer insisting no animals were injured in the making of this movie, including the fox, which will never leave its cage other than for a few shots in front of the camera. Instead, the hounds will chase a rag soaked with fox urine dragged through open fields and woods.

Having been chased through the wild myself—albeit by pygmies with poison arrows—I don't envy any animal in this predicament.

I still don't know how Willow plans on doing her scenes in Louboutin booties without breaking a leg. If so, will someone please shoot her to put her out of her misery? I'd gladly offer to do so, since no disclaimer regarding human injuries is required.

Having been to numerous jaunts of this ilk, besides passing along much-needed intel on a local asset with a lead on the Quorum, Dominic is also to be an extra. As such, he is properly turned out in the colors of a hunt master during the formal season: a black brimmed-helmet, ribbons points-down; a white four-fold stock tie pinned into place with a three-inch gold pin; buff leather gloves; black boots, buff breeches, and a canary-hued vest under his five-buttoned scarlet jacket.

The Devon hunt master is livid that Dominic's chummi-ness with Whitford has gotten him booted from his rightful position. To add insult to injury, Dominic gets to deliver the scene's sole line spoken by any extra, which is, "Tally-ho, away!"

Another thing that isn't quite winning him friends or influencing enemies among the hunters and the movie's production crew is the horse he's brought with him. Appropriately named Mr. Big, this bucking, snorting black stallion stands twenty-and-a-half hands. Needless to say, it dwarfs all the other horses, including the one to be ridden by Reed, who claims he'll look ridiculous on his own horse, and refuses to mount it.

In a way, I can see his point, since, technically, his horse is a pony.

Like its master, Mr. Big does not wait for a formal invitation to court the mares in his presence, but boldly mounts any of them within target of his extended sex organ. Those hunters riding atop the objects of his lust must leap off their steeds posthaste or risk finding themselves in the most unusual ménage-à-trois.

No surprise, Dominic is oblivious to the havoc around him.

On the other hand, Willow's animal instincts must be visually and odorously stimulated by it because she sidles up to Dominic and murmurs, "Well hung!"

He graces her with a smile. "So kind of you to notice. And you are?"

This should be a match made in heaven, so I might as well have dibs on playing yenta. "Lord Dominic Fleming, I'd like to introduce you to Willow Higginbotham, the star of *The Housewife Assassin's Handbook*—you know, the movie based on my life story. Sort of." I had to get that jibe in.

"Ah, so this little lady is your supposed doppelganger, is she?" His eyes roam approvingly over Willow's lithe physique. When he turns back to me, admiration morphs into doubt. "Oh! …Well, I'm sure the likeness is in the splendid performance. I say, old girl, the craft table certainly agrees with you!"

Any joke at another's expense—especially mine—sends Willow into a fit of giggles.

Yes, they should get along famously.

"Does it ever calm down?" Willow purrs, her eyes fixated on Mr. Big.

He raises a brow. "What would be the fun in that?"

Okay, I've had enough of this malarkey. I smack his arm. "Dominic, may I speak to you in private?"

He bows slightly to Willow before following me to a small copse of trees beyond the gathering. His manners are for naught. She hasn't taken her eyes off of Mr. Big. By the way her head is cocked, I'm sure she's making mental notes of the horse's mounting techniques.

"Dominic, you didn't come here to run a stud service for your horse. You're here to pass on information regarding a British asset."

"One doesn't preclude the other, now does it, my dear? And besides, if Acme goes under, both Mr. Big and I may be reduced to studding if I'm to make the mortgage on the Fleming ancestral estate." He shrugs. "No, no, you're right. Business before pleasure, eh?" He leans in conspiratorially. "The asset in question—Roger Cavanaugh—insisted on meeting you face to face before relaying his intel. As you can imagine, he's quite a nervous chap. But as it turns out, he hunts with the hounds—and has done so here, in fact, in

Devon—so my bringing him along has not raised suspicions in the least."

I nod. "Smart thinking. Where is he now?"

"I left him with Jack, at the tavern down in the village— the Railway Inn, on Beach Street."

I know it well. Like most of the cast, Jack and I have been put up in bungalows within the scenic little seaside town of Dawlish, just down the road from Castle Drogo. Some crew members, including Emma, have rooms there at the inn, above the pub.

On the other hand, since catching her in a clinch with Reed, Arnie has elected to bunk up the hill, at the South Devon Inn.

I can't say I blame him.

The wind has kicked up substantially in the past twenty minutes. Dominic glances skyward, where clouds are twirling around like bumper cars. "If Whitford wants to get any footage at all, he'd better get his cameras rolling now."

"Then I take it a hunt is called off when it rains?"

"My dear, of course not!" Dominic's look of pity makes me blush. "Granted, mud is a given, and silks are ruined in a rainstorm—not to mention a horse can break a leg if it slips. But it's all part and parcel of the sport. All the more reason to have a good seat, eh?" He angles his head to view my backside. "And you're more than amply covered in that regard. So, as we say, 'tally-ho!'"

A *veddy, veddy* smart move on his part—heading out before I wrench the whip out of his hand and use it on his own well-regarded rump.

The wind practically blows the car down the hill. If they

cancel the shoot today, the production will be further behind schedule than it already is, what with the explosion in Venezuela.

At least our time here has been without incident. One could get used to living in this pastorally beautiful country.

For the first time since we've been on the run, I'm feeling homesick.

Maybe Mr. Cavanaugh's news will be our ticket home.

I'M JUST A FEW BLOCKS FROM THE RAILWAY INN WHEN MY CAR passes Sebastian, just as he's about to get into his car and drive up to Castle Drogo. He's also in hunt attire, and carries a shotgun.

He waves to me, so I pull over to the curb.

"You're joining Jack and his guest, I presume?" he asks.

I hesitate to answer—not because I feel he's being nosy, but because no one is to know our covert assignations. But since he asks only out of politeness, the least I can do is answer in kind. "I've yet to meet the gentleman. He's an acquaintance of a friend."

"He and I have people in common, too. He's Franklin Crain, the barrister, is he not?" He motions to his hunt duds. "I've been called onto the set, or I would have stopped to reintroduce myself."

I shake my head. "No, his name is Roger Cavanaugh."

"Ah! My mistake. He and the man I know could pass for twins." He shakes his head, awed at the coincidence. "I presume the children are excited about the fox hunt."

"Indeed, they are. It's their first."

His grin disappears. "I still remember mine. Used to enjoy playing with our pack of hounds"—his eyes darken at the memory—"until that day."

"Oh? Why is that?"

"The hunt ended when the hounds cornered the fox. Tore him to pieces." He shudders. "My father insisted it is nature taking its course. 'We'll be overrun with the little buggers if they aren't hunted and thinned out,' he warned me. These days we drive the dogs crazy with a bit of fox scent on a rag. More humane, but he was right. Our farmers suffer for it. When the foxes take their chickens, they lose money." He shrugs. "It always comes down to that, doesn't it, money?"

I nod. "Sadly, yes. I'm always shocked at how indifferent we are to cruelty."

"It's the case they've made to reinstate the classic hunt, the animal rights activists be damned. Mark my words, the cruel always win." He tips his hat and starts up the road to join the shooting party.

I don't know why, but the conversation sent a shiver up my spine. Maybe it wasn't a great idea for the children to see a fox hunt after all. Too late now.

I take the last few yards to the inn at a trot. The sooner I meet Mr. Cavanaugh, the sooner I'll know if his lead pans out.

LIKE MOST BRITISH TAVERNS, THE RAILWAY INN IS DARK ON THE inside. After the moment it takes for my eyes to adjust to the lack of light, I spot Jack's long legs jutting out of a back booth.

The man sitting opposite him is slight, pale, and balding. Like Sebastian, he is wearing hunt attire. He stands and touches his hat's small brim as I take a seat beside Jack.

"Donna, Roger here was just telling me how he came to know our mutual friend, Carl."

My soon-to-be ex-husband's name causes the man to turn yet another shade closer to alabaster. "Well…not personally," he stutters. "You see, until quite recently, I was the night manager at the Royal International Club."

"It's a private establishment, in Mayfair," Jack explains. "By invitation only. You have to be referred, and seconded, by current members. Its membership is international in scope, primarily those who serve in some sort of diplomatic capacity."

Roger nods. "The man you call Carl Stone was known to me under a different name—Howard Betz. He'd been a member of the club for years, and frequented the club a few times a year, until an incident occurring in May of last year."

"What happened?" I ask.

Roger shifts uncomfortably on the booth's hard bench. "It was Mr. Betz's habit to arrive in the middle of the night. His other idiosyncrasies were to refuse housekeeping while in residence, and to demand the same room during each stay: on the top floor—the fourth—and on the side lacking the view most requested by guests. You see, the club is located on Cleveland Row, affording it an admirable view of the Green Park side of Buckingham Palace."

"How nice," I murmur.

Roger nods. "However, Mr. Betz's—I mean, Mr. Stone's desired room faces an alley. I presume it's how he got away with it."

"What do you mean?" Jack asks.

"He arrived around nine-thirty that evening, and retired promptly. At least, that was how it was to be presumed." Roger glances beyond the booth. Satisfied we're not being watched, he leans in. "However, I've come to believe he paid a visit to the room of another guest—a German gentleman who visited quite often."

"Whom would that be?" I ask.

"Johan Richter," Roger responds. "He was a member of the cabinet in his home country. That night, he'd been placed in a room on the third floor, also facing the alley, and immediately under that of Mr. Stone's. But unlike Mr. Stone, Herr Richter went out for the evening. However, the maid who came to turn down his bed—her name is Charlotte—found a man in the room. The gentleman claimed to be the room's registered occupant, allowed her to perform her duties, and tipped her on her way out."

"But you think the man wasn't Richter?"

"I know for a fact he wasn't. I'd ordered Herr Richter a hackney and watched him drive off in it. I was also on duty when he arrived back to the club, four hours later." He frowns. "The next morning, Herr Richter was found dead. The coroner ruled it a heart attack."

Jack and I exchange glances. Having induced "heart attacks" ourselves, we know it's a simple form of murder. The rapid injection of oxygen—say, one-hundred-and-fifty cc's—would be enough to stop his heart. Or for that matter replacing high-blood-pressure pills with far stronger ones than prescribed. I can go on and on.

"Even if foul play was the cause of death, how do you know for certain the man who Charlotte saw was indeed Carl Stone?" Jack asks.

"Herr Richter was known to be a loud snorer—hence the back room—and a sound sleeper." Roger gives the slightest of smiles. "He had requested a wake-up call for six. When he hadn't responded to it, I went to his room to wake him with a knock on the door. He didn't respond. I opened the room with the master key. I found him slumped in the chair, at the desk. He was still in evening attire. He succumbed while writing something. The handwriting was barely legible, but from what I could make out, it said, 'Clapham Sect.' Naturally, my first thought was that he'd succumbed to a heart attack. The coroner confirmed it. As is the club's policy, we took the body out of the building by way of the servant's elevator. The coroner's lorry was waiting in the back alley."

"Any idea what 'Clapham Sect' may mean? A neighborhood? Or perhaps another private club?" Jack asks.

Roger thinks for a moment. "No, I'm sorry I'm of no help to you there."

"I'm sorry, Roger, but I still don't see how any of this connects Carl to his death," I point out.

Roger turns to me. "Mr. Stone vacated his room a half-hour before the body was found. Charlotte happened to be leaving another guest's polished shoes outside his door on the fourth floor, when Mr. Stone left his room and rang for the elevator. Our staff is trained to be polite to guests, and to call them by name, if they recognize them. She nodded to

'Herr Richter,' but he ignored her—in fact, he tilted his hat so that she'd have a hard time seeing his face." Roger purses his lips. "She didn't think it odd at all that he was on another floor. After all, he may have been visiting another guest. However the next night, upon hearing of Herr Richter's untimely demise and that the time of death was put at two in the morning, she realized Mr. Stone wasn't the dead man after all. She was upset enough to mention it to me." Roger drops his head to study the pint of ale in front of him. "I told her she had to have been mistaken. In our positions we see a lot of people. And since there is no security footage of him leaving his room, let alone entering Herr Richter's, I suggested she consider herself mistaken."

To avoid detection, Carl would have climbed down from his window in order to enter Richter's room. He would have also altered any security feeds.

My heart is beating fast now. "Is Charlotte willing to confirm your account?"

Sadness darkens his eyes. "She died a few days later. She was hit in the middle of Brompton Road, by a tour bus, of all things. The incident so unnerved me that I gave notice immediately. I'm the night manager now at another club."

Frustrated, Jack taps the table with his fingertips. "Without her, we have nothing but hearsay and conjecture."

"Perhaps not." Roger pulls something from his vest pocket. "In his haste to leave the hotel, Mr. Stone left this in his room's trash can."

It is a clear, small plastic bag. The contents are a vial of pills. "It was already bagged, so no one else's fingerprints should be on it, if, in fact, his are there."

I pick up the bag. The vial has no label or markings. "The pills look like Digitalis, but we'll have to have them examined to be sure. If Richter was taking the drug for his heart and Carl knew it, we have the proof we need that Carl replaced his pills with a higher dosage, which could have killed him."

"The coroner will still have the dead man's vial in his case file. We can get it as well." Jack smiles. "Not exactly a slam dunk, but with your testimony, Roger, it certainly looks that way."

The night manager sighs his relief. "I truly liked Charlotte. When she mentioned her suspicions, I didn't take her seriously. If I had, perhaps I could have saved her life." He rises to his feet. "I'm sure I've missed the hunt scene, but so be it. It's all fantasy anyway, isn't it? The real world spills real blood."

We shake hands with him, but we let him leave first.

Jack places his hand over mine, which holds the plastic bag. "This is it—the last piece of the puzzle."

It's bad luck to presume we're out of the woods just yet, so I shush him with a kiss.

He's taking his sweet time disentangling himself from it. Fine by me.

Finally, I say, "I guess we should see what's happening at the hunt, too."

We're just a few miles from town when I realize we're not the only ones who are heading toward Castle Drogo. An ambulance, and several police cars pass us.

Not a good sign.

When we pull into the grounds of the estate, Jack runs up

to a constable, who is trying to keep the crowd at bay. "What's all the fuss?" he asks.

"An accidental shooting, I'm afraid—one of the young lasses involved in the production. She wasn't in the scene proper, but apparently she was hit by a stray shot."

There are only two 'young lasses' in the production—Mary and Rachel.

"But the actors weren't using real bullets," Jack reasons.

The constable shrugs. "Sadly, in this case, they were quite real."

As I race up the lane to the castle's grounds, my heart pounds in my chest. It could be from exertion, but more than likely I'll die from the dread that comes with realizing I've lost my daughter.

I pray to God to let me live at least until I get the chance to hold her in my arms one more time.

13

The Kids Are All Right

"It's hard enough to open your heart in this world. Don't make it harder."

—Mark Ruffalo, as "Paul"

IMAGINE THIS:

You're all dolled up in some bazillion-dollar gown, which was lent to you by a fashion designer, whose couture is reminiscent of the dresses worn, back in the day, by your favorite Barbie. How sweet is that?

You can tell the Academy of Arts and Sciences is about to announce the winner in the category in which you've been nominated because, suddenly, one of the eight live cameras roaming the Dolby Theatre is focused on you!

Immediately, you follow the lead of your competitors: you open your eyes wide, lick your lips, and turn up the star wattage on your smile.

You're also praying that you (a) don't break your beloved's wrist by holding it too tightly as you wait for your name to be called; (b) don't cry if your name isn't called, but smile valiantly and clap with some semblance of sincerity for the bitch who beat you; and if you win (c) you don't shout out some expletive, or trip on the hem of your much-too-expensive Barbie-worthy gown as you gallop to the stage, and (d) that you remember your well-practiced acceptance speech.

Let's just pretend you've won, okay? Here's the order in which you should thank all the little people who made you who you are today: (1) the Powers that Be (2) the film's producers, (3) the studio distributing the film, (4) your agent, (5) your make-up and hairdresser (6) your mother, wherever she is—hopefully, not stuck in the ladies' room— and (7) your significant other.

Should you forget any of the above, only one person on that list will forgive you. Sorry, if you can't figure out who I mean, you deserve the obscurity that will eventually come your way because of this one brain fart.

I'll give you one clue: it isn't your mother.

Now, go enjoy your hard-earned fame.

My daughter lays prostrate, face down on the ground in the mossy alcove beneath a tall tree.

Everything moves in slow motion: the wind, wafting through the branches above us; the clouds sitting low in the sky, dark and engorged; and the crowd hovering just beyond the tense ribbons of yellow police tape.

Those who seem to move the slowest of all are the paramedics working to revive a child, while those who pray hardest for her look on in horror.

Of course, I'm imagining this. In truth, all the life-saving maneuvers—chest pumping and oxygen masking and fluid infusion—are happening in real time.

Maybe if I heard something, anything, I could break the spell cast over me by this nightmare. But the ringing in my ears—the loud, shrill shriek—just won't stop.

That's okay. I'd much rather my precious Mary be in shock than have met with the fate of her dear friend Rachel, whose limp, dead body is the reason for my daughter's pain.

I wrap my body over hers. My attempt to shield Mary physically may provide her some comfort, but there is nothing I can do to stand between my daughter and the vision of seeing her friend's chest torn open by a bullet, or the memory that will linger for a lifetime of Rachel's shock, and final realization, that her life is now behind her.

Over and over I whisper, "You're safe, I promise, and I'm here for you…"

When she finally believes this is true, her screams end and she turns around so that I may cradle her in my arms.

"WHAT IS A 'SCI-FI' MOVIE?" TRISHA ASKS.

"It's about fun things that come from outer space," Jeff explains. "Or sometimes it takes place in the future. Trust me, you'll like it."

She wrinkles her nose. "Will the aliens speak English?"

He sighs. "Of course, silly! And in British accents, too.

Now, grab your rain coat. If we're going to catch the opening scenes, we have to leave now."

"Take an umbrella, too," I warn them. "It's starting to sprinkle."

At my behest, Jeff is taking Trisha to the local movie house, just down the street. Unfortunately, it only has one screen, so slim pickings. The film was produced here in Great Britain, and is one the children haven't seen. It isn't a great choice for a six- and an eleven-year-old, but it's better they be there than to see their sister like this.

"Who knows? Maybe it's something Addison can adapt," Jeff said. He isn't just trying to make the best of his role as Trisha's babysitter. He really means what he says.

I think he's found his calling.

The local doctor left a sedative for Mary. I had to force her to take it, so that she'd calm down.

Aunt Phyllis is in Mary's room, watching over her as she sleeps. My daughter cried until the sedative kicked in. Her shock over Rachel's death came out in self-loathing and blame. She was no more than a couple of yards from Rachel when the bullet hit her friend.

"Why am I still alive, when she's dead?" she asked herself, over and over.

I wait until Jeff and Trisha walk out the front door, and I've closed the door to Mary's room before asking Jack, "How is Addison handling this?"

"After he met with the police, he went back to his cottage in order to call Rachel's family, to break the news." Jack looks at his watch. "It's just now daybreak, Pacific Time."

"I don't envy him the task. As for her parents…" My voice trails off.

Jack puts his arm around my waist. He knows what I'm thinking—no parent wants to go through the horror of hearing the news of his or her child's death.

"I'm sure Addison is weighing the consequences of her death on the picture's viability," Jack brushes my forehead with his lips. Does he feel me trembling? He must because he holds me tighter, as if he'll never let me go.

That would be fine with me.

"Since all of Rachel's scenes were completed as of yesterday, no rewrites are needed, so it won't affect the production schedule," I reason out loud. "And, as odd as it seems, her devoted fans will want to see her final project, if only to connect with her one last time. I can see why. She was luminous on the big screen. It's a shame she never fulfilled her potential."

"Sebastian wrote a great script, and Whitford knows what he's doing with it. But you're right. As far as the cast is concerned, the only reason to see this movie is because of Rachel." Jack shrugs. "Right now, the biggest issue facing the production is the stance of its insurance underwriters. Between the explosion in Venezuela that took the lives of the two stunt doubles and now a featured actor's death on the set, the underwriter may have all the reason it needs to pull the plug on the production." He takes his cell phone out of his pocket. "Speaking of which, I should check in with Arnie. He's still at the crime scene, assessing it with the police." A moment later, he's murmuring instructions to Arnie.

When he hangs up, he turns back to me. "Chad and Whitford have released all the firearms to the investigators, as have the hunt club members who played extras and were allowed to use their personal guns. The Special Effects crew insists each and every gun, both real and props, was checked and double-checked to assure the ammunition in the chamber was only blanks."

"But if the shooter wasn't a cast member or movie extra, whose gun was it, and why would they shoot Rachel?" I ask.

"Good question. I think I'll do a bit of snooping on my own."

The rain is now coming down in sheets. I walk over with his coat, a hat, and an umbrella. "This weather is going to make it harder to find clues in the woods, if that's where you're going."

My consideration earns me a furtive kiss.

He checks the chamber of his HK P11. The bullets in it are real.

Best yet, one of the gun's highly touted features is that it actually shoots underwater. Considering Dawlish's flood advisory and the way it's pouring outside, he may get the chance to find out for himself if that's true.

He and his gun may get soaked, but he'll be safer than whoever killed Rachel.

MARY SLEPT ONLY TWO HOURS. JACK IS STILL NOT BACK, BUT he's phoned to give me updates on the ballistics reports as they come in. So far, the killer's weapon hasn't been identified.

Jeff and Trisha are back from the movie. While they help Aunt Phyllis prepare dinner, I sit with Mary. I'm relieved she seems to want to talk about what happened almost as badly as I want to hear about it. Her sobs trickle out between every other sentence. I hold her hand. It's a small comfort, but maybe it will get her through the ordeal of reliving her memories.

"It's all my fault," she laments. "Rachel thought it would be fun to cut through the woods and follow the dogs. But she wouldn't have done it by herself if I'd said no."

"Wasn't she more interested in watching the scene being shot?"

Mary looks at me as if I'm the one having the breakdown. "No way! Rachel could not have cared less about it. The fact that Willow and Reed are so unprofessional drove her crazy. And overall, she hated action movies. She would have preferred to attach herself to a small independent film. The only reason she accepted the role in this movie was so that she could get on Sebastian's radar." She closes her eyes. "For the next season of *Bloomsbury* he's writing in a big part for an American woman, exactly her age."

"Is that what he told her?"

She shakes her head. "She read it in the *Wrap*. She felt the exposure would be incredible for her. She was dying to move to England so that she could take on some stronger female roles. 'Here, they don't just hire you for your looks,' is how she put it."

"Why didn't she just ask Sebastian if she could audition for the role?" I ask.

"She did. He said he'd certainly consider it. He was always flirting with her, so she thought he meant it. But… well, I don't think so. Frankly, I think he was leading her on to…you know, just to date her."

I've seen that side of Sebastian. He can turn on the charm when he wants something. When he gets it, he goes his merry way.

"Why do you feel he wasn't being honest with her?"

Mary frowns. "He takes a full set of bound copies of each episode's teleplay with him wherever he goes. She asked him if she could read them. She wanted to learn them backward and forward. But he wouldn't lend them to her. He said he needed them for research while he worked on next season's scripts. But she was determined to change his mind, so that he wouldn't see her as just another 'silly American actress.' She knew about his—well, about his 'dates' with Willow."

No surprise there. So Emma's scuttlebutt was right and Willow was sleeping her way through the whole cast and crew!

"Rachel was desperate to impress Sebastian before she left tomorrow," she continues. "He finally consented to hear her read. She was even more determined than ever to get her hands on the scripts. She knew the desk clerk at the inn where Sebastian was staying had a crush on her. The clerk gave her a skeleton key so that we could sneak into Sebastian's room and grab a script whenever we wanted one. She'd memorize it, then we'd slip it back into his room. Soon, she had the lines all memorized." Tears roll down her cheeks. "She auditioned yesterday. She told me she pulled out all the stops. She knew he was impressed with her knowledge of the show, and with the insights she had on all the characters. He was even laughing at her imitations of some of them, calling them spot on. She thought she had the role in the bag." She sighs. "I think it's why she confessed about our break-ins to him."

I sigh. "I presume he didn't take it well."

"You can say that again!" She shudders at the thought. "She said he turned purple, he was so angry. He yelled at her, telling her that there were no copies in circulation for a reason—because they were historic, and that every word in the script was there for a reason. He made her assure him that she'd returned all of them, and he threatened to ruin her if she were lying."

"What a pompous ass," I mutter.

"She thought so, too." She shrugs. "For the most part, he's right. The actors follow the script verbatim—that is, except for the character of Virginia Woolf. Every now and then she'll alter a line or two."

That's certainly strange. "How do you know this?" I ask her.

"It was part of Rachel's obsession with *Bloomsbury*. After getting her hands on a script, we'd compare them to the actual episodes, which we'd stream on Netflix. She wanted to see how the actors read their lines—their tone, the inflections they'd use, that sort of thing."

"Was there anything else that stood out to you, or to Rachel, regarding the scenes in which the lines were changed? For example, did it take place on a particular set, at the same time within the course of the show?"

"No, not that I can remember." But then Mary hesitates and a strange look comes over her face. "Wait! Yes, there was one other thing Rachel noticed. Whenever a line change occurred, the phrase 'the Apostles' was substituted for another—'the Clapham Sect.' At first I didn't get it, but Rachel explained that both were elite social cliques for really smart people who the Bloomsbury Group respected—Mom, what's wrong? You look as if you've seen a ghost!"

She's right—it's the ghost of Johan Richter.

Sebastian is a Quorum operative.

Somehow, the scripts fit into the equation—

Oh my god—the shows are syndicated throughout the world. Could he be using the shows to relay messages to the terrorist cells controlled by the Quorum?

The only way to verify this is to get my hands on the scripts, and compare them to the actual episodes.

"I...I'm just so surprised Rachel picked up on something so—so insignificant," I say as nonchalantly as possible, but in truth, the last thing I want for Mary to learn is the significance of those words in our lives.

"Rachel was really smart in so many ways. Her attention to small details was amazing." Mary's eyes cloud up again. "And now she's gone."

I pat her arm. "You can't blame yourself, Mary. You both just happened to be in the wrong place at the wrong time."

"I should have never let her walk so far ahead of me! If the hunter had seen both of us, perhaps he wouldn't have shot her." Her voice is practically a whisper.

I guess the sedative is still doing its magic. I have to ask her one more question before she drifts off to sleep. "Mary, do you know if she still has any of the scripts?"

"Yes…one…" Her eyelids are too heavy now.

The next thing I know, she's snoring.

I wrap the blanket around her and give my sweet girl a kiss on the forehead.

If Sebastian checks his scripts, he may realize one is missing. He'll be searching Rachel's room for it.

I've got to get it before he does, so that we have the proof we need.

I make Aunt Phyllis promise to keep the doors locked to anyone besides Jack, Arnie, Emma or me. She has Jeff and Trisha set up in front of the cozy fireplace, roasting marshmallows. Considering the storm slamming up against the house, no one should be outside unless his or her life depends on it.

Mine does.

I brace myself for whatever awaits me, slamming the door behind me.

14

Lady Killer

"Too many hurricanes, blow you right out of bed. Wake up in the morning and find a boat in your lap."

James Cagney, as "Dan Quigley"

[*FINAL SCENE IN THE SCREENPLAY FOR* THE HOUSEWIFE Assassin's Handbook]

CUT TO:

Ext. Railroad Bridge – Night

The camera captures DONNA STONE's face as she walks slowly along the RAILROAD TRACKS on a SEAWALL, clinging to a SEASIDE CLIFF.

SFX: TRAIN WHISTLE

From over her shoulder a TRAIN can be seen coming down the tracks. She is silhouetted in its HEADLIGHT.

SFX: TRAIN WHISTLE – tooting frantically, warning her it can't stop.

She ignores it —

Until it's just fifty feet away —

Which is when she turns around, whips out a GUN, and aims it directly at the train's headlight —

And fires right at it.

SFX: Glass breaking as the headlight shatters, the SQUEAL of BRAKES, the CRASH of STEEL upon STEEL —

But Donna stands her ground as the train jumps the track —

Falling into the lake, engine first.

Donna stares down, as the train's CABOOSE disappears under the surface of the water. A few BUBBLES roil to the surface.

She pulls a CELL PHONE out of her pocket and hits a BUTTON on it:

DONNA
Mission accomplished.

She continues her stroll down the track.

THE END

BECAUSE SHE WAS PART OF THE FEATURED CAST, RACHEL WAS given a townhouse with a spectacular view of Dawlish's seawall, which holds up a pedestrian promenade along the railway track, at the ocean's edge.

With a gale force of over a hundred miles an hour, the

storm slams into the shore every few seconds and whips the waves into walls of churning froth rising as high as twenty feet.

It takes all my might to move forward. To do so, I'm practically walking sideways and clinging to anything that looks as if it can hold me on my quest to reach the dead girl's doorway.

Only someone desperate would be out in this weather.

I resemble that remark.

Unfortunately, so does Sebastian.

I'm a block from my destination when another wave rises beyond the seawall, drenching me in its spray. My curses can't be heard in the howling wind. I realize this is a good thing when I see Sebastian coming out of Rachel's doorway.

When he turns around, he sees me, too.

He freezes. Then he smiles.

Until he sees the gun in my hand.

I see something, too, in the crux of his arm—a script, wrapped in a plastic sack.

"Hand it over!" I scream over the storm's moan.

"Sorry, but it's got a date with a match, just like all the others," he shouts back.

Aw hell, he's already burned the rest of them.

A bullet is much faster than a woman drenched to the bone and walking in a pair of soggy sneakers. I raise my gun to fire—

Only for it to get slapped out of my hand by a mammoth wave.

It also tosses me down and flips me over.

I resurface, spewing salt water. By the time I'm back on my feet, the gun is long gone.

Worse yet, Sebastian is nowhere to be seen. Was he washed away, too? I scour the street, but the curtains of rain slapping me in the face make it next to impossible to make out anything beyond a few feet in front of me.

I run to Rachel's doorway, to see if he was able to make it back inside. I've almost reached it when something broadsides me—

Or I should say someone. Sebastian has me on the ground, and under the water.

It may not be ladylike to twist a gentleman's nutsack, then again he's not much of a gentleman if he's shoved the lady's head into a briny puddle. I'm surprised Sebastian's howl can be heard above the shrieking storm, but it just goes to show you that men are sensitive, too—at least where it counts the most.

To them.

While he rolls on the ground in pain, I go for the script—

But the wind blows and whips it just beyond my reach. It glides on a low tailwind toward the seawall. I duck and dive for the script, but it bobs and weaves and skids just out of reach.

I luck out when it drops onto the tracks. I reach down to grab it—

But Sebastian shoves me down.

As I fall onto the track, my foot gets caught under one of the rails.

Sebastian holds up the script triumphantly in one hand.

The other hand holds my gun.

He's only a few feet away, and I'm a sitting duck.

He aims the gun at my head.

I brace myself with both hands on the rail and hold my breath in anticipation—

Of the thirty-foot wall of water about to wash over us.

He doesn't see it coming.

But he sees the fear in my eyes.

By the time he turns around, it's too late.

As the wave crashes down upon us, I hold my breath, and hold on for dear life.

I try not to think of what is taking place around me, above me, or below me. I am slammed from all sides—not just by the water, but all things that take flight in the wake of unexpected storms: branches, flower pots, garbage, even bicycles. I envision the rumbling in my ears to be a train headed our way, but I know that's impossible because the trains would have been cancelled in a storm of this magnitude.

So then, why is the track shaking violently?

I force my eyes open, only to find that while I've been clinging to the track, it is hanging practically in thin air, suspended on tall spindly metal pylons.

The rest of the seawall has been washed out to sea.

So has Sebastian. I see him on his back. His dead man's float is the real thing.

The plastic bag holding the script stays afloat, too—a white spec ebbing toward a gunmetal gray horizon.

A moment later, both dip beneath the waves.

I crawl, crablike, over the tracks and thin air, until I reach the roadway that used to hug the seawall.

I pray Jack made it back to the children in one piece.

If he did and I'm not there, he'll be worried out of his mind.

I run back to our cottage, as fast as the wind will allow.

Suddenly, I miss Hilldale.

15

Apocalypse Now

"What do you call it when the assassins accuse the assassin? A lie. A lie, and we have to be merciful."

Marlon Brando, as "Kurtz"

YOU CAN CERTAINLY GLEAN A FEW GREAT BEAUTY TIPS BY hanging around the make-up trailer on a movie set. Here are a few that will make you look younger, perkier, and (dare I say it?) even more beautiful than you already are:

- *Tip #1: There are around twenty basic makeup foundations, which come in both oil and water bases. The key is finding the shade that best matches your skin tone, or the hue that works best to transform you into the character. Mix two shades if necessary.*

However, if you end up with one that is too dark, you're the

Creature from the Black Lagoon. Too light, and you're Lily Munster. Bottom line: Experiment until you get it right.

- *Tip #2: Use a make-up mirror with light settings that will emulate the lighting used on the set, be it sunlight, fluorescent, or incandescent. This avoids making you look like a monster—too green, like Frankenstein, or in partial shadow, like a vampire.*
- *Tip #3: Always outline the lips with a pencil or a liner before filling in with a lipstick. However, never use a lipstick with a blue hue, unless you want to come off like the living dead.*

Do you see a pattern here? The goal is to stay away from anything that will make others balk, gag, or run when they see you—

Unless the script calls for it.

If it does, change agents, because obviously, this one doesn't see you as you see yourself.

"Uh oh!" Jeff looks up from his iPad, where he's surfing the industry trades between reading the latest uploaded scripts in *The Black List.*

My way of trying to forget the fact that the one thing that might have bought us diplomatic immunity with the British Government is now a soggy block of pulp at the bottom of the English Channel is to braid Trisha's unruly hair. But any under-the-breath exclamation by a child containing my genetic make-up gives me cause to pause. "Why do you say that?"

He shrugs. "The rumors are flying, both on the set and off." He clicks on the tablet's toolbar and his screen changes to the *Deadline Hollywood* banner. One of the banner sliders reads, *Housewife Assassin Slays Screenwriter.*

Oh, heck.

I snatch the device out of his hand and scan the article.

Yes, it's me.

And yes, the film footage was apparently shot during my altercation with Sebastian—at the exact moment he fell to his death.

Who the hell took it, and why?

Did the same person send it to the media?

The caption accompanying it reads, "This video clip, sent to *Deadline Hollywood* by an unnamed source, shows an anonymous woman with Gillingham when he drowned. What is not clear in the video is who she is, and why they chose to rehearse this action scene during the biggest storm to hit the English Coast in forty years. However, the footage clearly shows some fancy footwork on the mystery woman's part, at least up until the time when Gillingham realizes he's caused her to fall. Tragically, as he reaches to help her up with the prop gun, he is washed out to sea. Considering the Royal Family's zeal for *Bloomsbury*, it is no wonder the argument for posthumous knighthoods has been revived."

I thank God the camera was too far away to show my face. Not that Carl scans Tinseltown industry trade rags, but if he did, this headline, coupled with the photo and his knowledge of Sebastian's whereabouts, might make him curious enough to have his tech team blow up the photo so that he can see my face more clearly.

We might be arrested at any moment.

I turn to my aunt. "Did you have anything to do with this?"

She looks up from her knitting. "Honey, you know very well my paparazzi days are over."

"That's only because Willow's assistant, Augusta, tossed your cell phone in the toilet, and you were told you'd be banned from the set. Tell me the truth, Aunt Phyllis—did you take this video with one of my children's phones?"

The half-knitted sweater in her lap falls to the floor as she springs to her feet. "I'm not even going to justify that remark with another answer, since I've just given you one. Take it or leave it!"

She stalks off with tears in her eyes.

"Mommy, why are you being so mean to Aunt Phyllis?" Trisha glares at me as she runs after her.

I should apologize and calm them both down, but right now, every second counts, so instead I head for the door, iPad in hand.

"Mom...what's wrong?" Jeff frowns. "Where are you going with that? Addison expects coverage on at least three scripts by dinner time!"

"Ask Mary if you can borrow her iPad."

"Only if he promises not to leave cookie crumbs all over it, like last time," Mary mutters from the couch. She's still in her pajamas, and has a blanket over her head. The way she's mourning Rachel's death has me worried about my eldest.

"Please, Jeff, just take care of your sisters. Don't answer the door, unless it's either your father or me."

I've got to find Jack. If we can't do damage control on this, it may be time to hit the road again.

I CAN'T FIND JACK ANYWHERE. I TEXT ABU TO SEE IF THEY'RE together, but get back, *Nope, haven't seen him.*

Maybe he's with Emma or Arnie.

I seek out Arnie first. I find him with the rest of the special effects crew and Chad, the second unit director, assessing the damage the storm has done to the railroad tracks, where the next scene is to be shot. I've arrived just in time to hear Chad exclaim, "It'll take the British government months to rebuild it! Either we have to find another location, and pronto, or we'll have to scrap the scene altogether."

Arnie is upset about something. It's written all over his face. Finally, he notices that I'm trying to wave him over and he heads towards me.

"Arnie, we're in very big trouble! Someone took a video of Sebastian attacking me on the tracks before he was hit by the wave that took him out to sea. The person then sent it to *Deadline Hollywood*! If Carl sees it and recognizes it as me, the Feds will come for us. I can't find Jack anywhere, to warn him. Have you seen him?"

All the color drains out of Arnie's face. He shakes his head slowly. "No, I haven't seen him all morning, but" —he stares down at his feet, as if they hold the words that are alluding him—"I was the one who took the film footage."

"What? ...But why?"

"I guess I was trying to impress Chad. With the velocity of the storm due our way, I felt we could take advantage of having some truly spectacular waterworks on the tracks to use as cutaway footage for the train scene. So, I set up a digital camera with a telephoto lens on the summit of the hill, pointed it at the spot I knew he'd want—where the track is closest to the sea wall—and let it run all afternoon, when the storm rolled in. A few hours later, I came back to retrieve the camera, but it was gone! I thought it had blown away or something."

"Obviously not. Now we have to find out who stole it, reviewed the footage, and sent it out to the media."

"Donna, if I'd known you'd end up there with Sebastian—"

I put my hand on his shoulder. I realize he's upset with Emma's infatuation with Reed and has been trying to keep himself busy so that he doesn't have to think about it. "I don't blame you, Arnie. At the time, none of us knew Sebastian's true allegiances. The camera just happened to be at the right place at the wrong time. Right now, I need to find Jack so that he can assess the damage. If we split up, maybe one of us will run into him. I'm on my way to the make-up trailer to see if Emma has seen him."

"I'll see if he's with Addison, or maybe Whitford." He's off, heading toward the soundstage.

Every second counts. We both know it.

~

I TAP ON THE DOOR OF THE MAKE-UP TRAILER. NO ONE answers, but I heard angry voices just a moment before.

It's all the reason I need to bang on the door until someone opens it.

Emma's head pops out. Her eyes are red and puffy. "Donna! What are you doing here?"

Has she been crying? It's been a while since we've talked one-on-one. I need to learn to be a better friend—certainly before I end up in a prison cell. Note to self: stock up on cartons of cigs for your new besties, so that you have some-thing to trade for shivs. "Emma, sorry to interrupt, but I'm looking for Jack. Have you seen him?"

She looks back anxiously. When she faces me again, she shakes her head.

Something isn't right.

"We need to talk." Before she knows it, I've pushed past her, into the trailer. "Somehow the tabloids got ahold of—"

It's not Jack, but Reed, standing on the far side of the room. His arms are crossed at his chest and he's scowling.

I turn back around to Emma. "I'm sorry to intrude. Is…is everything okay?"

Emma bursts into tears.

I guess I have my answer.

He tries to push past me as he heads for the door, but I step out in front of him. "What the hell did you do to her?"

He raises his hands, in mock defense. Smirking, he mutters, "She's a big girl. She can take care of herself. And if she won't, she'll be hearing from my attorney." He shoves past me.

But he doesn't get far.

When I yank the floor runner out from under him, he trips and falls on his knees with a yelp.

"Tsk, tsk! How clumsy of you, Reed," I murmur. "You should watch your step."

He staggers to his feet. Angrily, he looks back at me, but he's smart enough to keep his mouth shut.

The door slams behind him.

I turn to Emma. "What did he mean by that?"

She collapses into one of the make-up chairs. "I...I'm late —over a week now. It's not at all like me. Donna, I'm pregnant!"

I guess Arnie was right to be jealous. "What are you going to do about it?"

"I don't know! Reed wants me to—to get rid of it!" Her words come out in fits and starts because she's crying so hard. "If I did, I don't know if I could live with myself. But, if I don't, it changes everything! Donna, I don't know if I'm ready to be a mother! I don't know if...if I can tell Arnie." She covers her face with her hands.

I bend down in order to wrap my arms around her. Arnie will be heartbroken. We both know it.

Every action has a consequence. In my case, I've still got to figure out if my confrontation with Sebastian has put my family and me in danger, and the sooner, the better. But Emma is my friend, and she needs me now.

Finally Emma rises from the chair. As she pats her eyes dry with a tissue, she asks, "Why are you looking for Jack?"

"Some film footage taken here has been released to the media, and I'm in it. We may have to take off. Any ideas where he may be?"

"I presume he's with Willow." She hesitates. Finally she murmurs, "When she was getting made up for her next scene, she called him and asked if he'd join her in her cottage, during the lunch break."

"Did she say why?"

Emma must pick up on my anger because she pauses before saying, "Well, to be honest, she said she had something to show him…something that she thought he'd be very interested in seeing."

I'll just bet she does.

Jack has made it quite clear, even to Willow, that he finds her annoying. She's been so offended that now she makes it a point to blow him off, every chance she gets.

Sorry, poor choice of words, considering her previous film experience.

If she's the one who stole the camera to use it to blackmail me, certainly Jack will be doing everything he can to make her change her mind—including kowtowing to her desire to kiss and make up.

Nope, not going to happen.

I give Emma a peck on the cheek and run out the door.

For some reason, Willow is giggling.

What the heck is so funny?

I'm sure as hell going to find out.

Just as I reach up to knock on the door of the star's cottage, Augusta, Willow's assistant-from-Hades, appears, seemingly out of nowhere. "Can I help you?"

"Willow wants to see me."

"I doubt it. She's busy, if you catch my drift." And to make sure I do, she shoves me to one side, so that she can block my path.

I don't have time for polite chitchat. So that she gets this message loud and clear, I slam her up against the cottage wall and hold her there with my forearm against her throat. "Yes, I know she's 'busy'—*with my husband.*"

"Then he should consider himself a lucky guy," she snorts. "Give him some space. He came to negotiate on your behalf."

From the giggles we hear, Jack is doing a piss poor job of it.

At least now I know it was Willow who took the camera and sent the film clip to *Deadline.*

I grab Augusta by the scruff of her turtleneck and pull her inside with me.

"Donna, trust me, it's not what you think," Jack pleads with me.

It sure as hell better not be.

Both of them are on the floor—on their backs, and panting heavily. Their thighs are entwined. He holds her foot in one hand, at the toes.

"What the hell?" Augusta yells. Why, she's even angrier than me.

But now that I see the situation, I can forgive him. To prove it, I bend down and kiss him. "Great technique."

"You people are sickos!" Augusta yanks Willow up off the ground and shoves her onto the bed.

Jack jumps to his feet and jerks her away. "Whoa, lady! Just what do you think you're doing?"

"I should be asking you the same question," she snarls at him.

That's it for me. Obviously a demonstration is in order.

An elbow to the gut has Augusta bowing. A kick behind her knees makes her fold, like a deck of cards, onto the ground—chest down, geisha-style. A second later I'm cuddling her in a bear hug. Give me another second and I've hooked my arm around her ankle and rolled her onto her back along with me.

Her leg is now trapped in the crook of my knee. When I pull her toes forward, she groans in agony.

"It's a Jiu-Jitsu move, you moron. It's called a calf slicer."

"Oh! Is that how it's supposed to look?" Willow seems disappointed. "It's not at all sexy."

"No?" Augusta gasps. "I dunno. I can see the potential."

Jack shakes his head in resignation. "It's not supposed to be sexy. It's a maneuver to stop someone from hurting you." He gives me a hand up.

"Why the hell were you learning it, anyway?" Augusta rubs her bruised toes.

"Don't be stupid, Augusta," Willow sighs. "I've got to live up to my soon-to-be new reputation as a female action star."

I grab Willow's arm. "So it was you who stole the camera, and leaked the film clip to the press—just to further your career!"

"Get real! I don't do rainstorms. Can you imagine what that would do to my hair?" She wrenches her arm from my grip. "I didn't even know about the incident until I got a call from my agent at CAA, just an hour ago. Every action film director in town is calling to find out if I'm the mystery woman, and if so, am I doing my own stunts? How Angelina Jolie is that?" She flexes a muscle and strikes a pose for the mirror. "CAA is dying for me to confirm it. The second I do, I'll be cast in the role of the Wasp for the next Avengers film. Isn't that exciting?"

Augusta furrows her brow. "But...I thought the only reason you wanted to take this film was to impress Sebastian with your ability to play a Brit, and get cast in *Bloomsbury*."

"Yeah, well, that was when I thought this film was going to bomb—and before Sebastian fell off the edge of the earth." She shrugs. "As much as I'd like to take on *Bloomsbury* and Shakespeare and Shaw and all the other highbrow roles, I'd much rather live somewhere I can get a tan—not to mention earn the big bucks that come with an action tentpole film with sequel potential."

Why, the ungrateful hussy! Without my biopic, she'd still be doing inane rom-coms. "Why would you want to be just another *Avenger* super hero when the *Housewife Assassin* series will go on forever? Addison has a six-picture arc set for the franchise."

She rolls her eyes. "I wouldn't count on it. Between Rachel and Sebastian's deaths—not to mention the explosion on the set in Venezuela—the insurance company told Sebastian to pull the plug on the picture. Whitford is gathering up the cast and crew now, to let them know." Her mouth droops into a pout. "I'd already be out of here, except for the fact that your husband is playing hardball. He won't let me confirm that I'm the woman in the video."

I look at Jack as if he's crazy. Of course he should let her take credit for pushing Sebastian into a watery grave—unless he's looking forward to visiting me in the hoosegow.

Then again, his adorable mug is plastered on Wanted posters, too. If he showed up for even one conjugal visit, the guards might slap him in irons.

I'm just about to remind him of this when Willow says, "If I trade you my Malibu place for the rights to tell the world I'm the woman doing the stunt in the film, can we call it even?"

Jack frowns as if she's got him over a barrel. "I don't know. What do you think, my lady love?"

I purse my lips. "The traffic is hell on PCH...but what the heck. The kids love the beach. I say go for it."

He nods toward the iPad in my hand. "Willow, give me a second to draft something for you to sign, so that it's all nice and legal."

She clasps her hands gleefully. But a moment later, her smile fades. She must be furrowing her brow, but it's hard for me to tell because it's practically a Kabuki mask, what with all the Botox in her forehead. "I'll still need someone to teach me all those cool martial arts moves—on the sly, that is." She bats her eyes at Jack. "Can we make that part of the deal, too?"

"No can do. We may be traveling a lot this year."

That's putting it mildly.

"But I'll tell you what," Jack goes on, "why don't I hook

you up with one of our colleagues, Dominic Fleming? He's very discreet, and he's got some moves that you'll really enjoy. I promise."

"The lord with the hung horse? Hmmm, yes, he'll do quite nicely! We'll practice at my Santa Barbara ranch. He can bring Big Boy if he wants. I could watch that stud all day long." She grabs the iPad and signs with a flourish. She snaps her fingers at Augusta. "Let's get packing, before another rainstorm rolls in."

At least one more shit storm has been diverted.

I'm out the door, with Jack right behind me.

16

Love Story

"Love means never having to say you're sorry."

Ali McGraw, as "Jennifer Cavilleri"

AT THEIR WORST, STAGE KISSES LOOK AWKWARD. AT THE VERY worst, they make the audience feel as uncomfortable as the actors. Here are four tips on how to make kissing another actor look as natural as a real-life smooch:

First, practice your kisses at every rehearsal. A lot of actors are so embarrassed about having to kiss a stranger that they wait until the very last rehearsal. By then, it's too late to change what may be natural with you and your normal squeeze, but is so wrong here. Don't be shy! Remember, practice makes perfect!

Next, really kiss. Don't just touch lips, or give your stage partner a quick peck. Get into it! You can't fake it.

Now, take your clothes off. I'm being serious! A kiss will seem tamer if you see each other naked.

And finally, have sex with your stage partner. Not fake porn sex. I mean really get down and dirty. Yes, I thoroughly understand that you're not starring in a blue film. But, since the point is to be as authentic as possible, after establishing this intimacy between you, the kissing part is second nature.

My goodness, the things we community theater actors do for our art!

FROM ALL THE LONG FACES WE PASS ON THE WAY TO OUR bungalow, I take it that Addison's news is a big blow to everyone.

We get a chance to hear it ourselves when we find Addison outside our door. He nods when he sees us. "I guess you heard that a clip of *The Housewife Assassin's Handbook* made it onto *Deadline Hollywood.*"

"Yes. And so did Willow. She's so excited she's calling the press to confirm her skills of derring-do," Jack says.

"Her double won't own up to it, so she must be telling the truth," Addison smirks. "Who knew she had it in her? She squeals every time she breaks a nail. Go figure."

"Addison, do you have any idea who forwarded the clip to *Deadline?*"

He laughs. "Who do you think sent it?" He jabs a thumb at his chest.

I don't get it. "But...why?"

"I needed something to counter all the bad publicity we were getting. Think about it. This was Rachel's last role. Her fans would have been lining up around the block to see the film! And *Bloomsbury* fans would have come in droves, too—especially if I'd been able to convince Whitford to incorporate Sebastian's death footage into the climax scene—you know, as an 'homage,' right?"

"Wrong," I mutter. Some homage!

And what if someone recognized me?

The fact that I'm horrified at the thought doesn't faze him. He shrugs. "I guess Whitford thought so, too. He threatened to walk off the picture. Said doing it would be 'macabre.' Damn artistic types! Can't live with them, can't live without 'em." He rolls his eyes. "I thought releasing the clip to*Deadline*, then following up with an unsubstantiated rumor that Willow did all her own stunts—including that one—would create the kind of buzz we need to keep the investors happy. I guess I'm too smart for my own britches. I didn't think it would cause the insurance company to back out." He shrugs. "That's okay. There may be a private investor willing to see it completed. Then I'll round up the team, tell them we're doing it in memory of our fallen comrades in arms."

"And for investors," Jack mutters under his breath.

Addison's face falls. He's wounded. "Hey, I have a heart. But I've also got to eat."

From what I've seen, he's wrong on both counts.

"Speaking of which," Jack says, "the clause in our contract—you know, about fees for sequels—I presume this kills any chance to collect them."

Addison laughs. "Don't sweat it. The money is still yours."

Jack looks as stunned as I feel.

"Not to look a gift horse in the mouth or anything, but how is this possible?" I ask.

"Because GWI—" Addison's voice trails off. "Let's just say I drove a hard bargain with my investors on your behalf, and it paid off." He looks up at the sky. Once again the sun has disappeared behind thick gray clouds. "I'm ready to get back to sunny California. Oh, and tell your son I expect that coverage before we're wheels up, in two hours."

He shuffles off.

We won't be on the plane. From what he just let slip, I think he's well aware of this.

Frankly, with no *Bloomsbury* script to give Ryan so that he can get back into MI6's good graces, the immunity we were looking for here in England is out of our reach.

It's truly a shame.

Next stop for us: Croatia. It's one of the few countries that doesn't have an extradition treaty with the US.

I'll download a Croatian Berlitz course for the kids. Seriously, I'll do anything to get out of homeschooling them.

"CROATIA?" THE THOUGHT OF GOING TO YET ANOTHER FOREIGN land has finally shaken Mary out of her malaise. "I don't get it! If the filming is done, why can't we just go home?"

Jack sits on the bed beside her. "My company needs me there."

"So go, send us a few postcards. But the rest of us want to go home—don't we?" She looks around the room.

"I wouldn't mind going home," Jeff pipes up. "Addison

has already offered me an internship at his production company."

"I don't think so," I say firmly. "All that means is you'll do a ton of work without getting paid."

Jeff shrugs. "Hey, it's show biz. Most players get their start in the mailroom. At least I'm already reading scripts."

"See? So far, two of us are ready to go home!" Mary jumps out of the bed in order to kneel in front of her little sister and look her in the eye. "How about you, Trisha? Wouldn't you like to go home and see Miss McGonagall, and all your friends?"

Trisha nods slowly. "Yes…but not if Mom and Dad can't come with us. I don't like it when they go away."

Mary frowns. "They'll come with us if we have the majority vote."

"This isn't a democracy. It's a family, which means parents decide what is best for the family as a whole," I warn her. "And right now, being somewhere other than Hilldale is best for all of us."

Aunt Phyllis throws her knitting into the bag at her feet. "Donna, dear, I think it's wonderful that the two of you want to give the family all these wonderful experiences. Truly, I do. But maybe it would be a better thing for them when they're older and they can appreciate it. Here's a thought! Why not consider making this a 'me time' getaway, just for the two of you? I'll be more than happy to move in and stay with the children until you're ready to come home again."

Ah, if only she knew: I'm ready now.

From the disappointed glances Mary and Jeff exchange, I

presume they aren't too thrilled about the compromise Aunt Phyllis has just offered us. Still, they keep their mouths shut.

Trisha is sobbing now. "I want Mommy and Daddy to stay with us."

Tears soften Mary's eyes, too. She walks over to me. "Be honest with us, Mom. Why won't you and Dad come home with us?"

She's right. I should always be honest with them.

There's only one way in which to learn how they'll react: *Just tell them.*

And to do it quickly, like pulling a Band-Aid from a wound.

The fact we're innocent doesn't mitigate the fact that the adults they love and trust most are fugitives from the law.

On the upside, once the shock and awe wears off, they'll be so mortified at the thought that their friends know, but they'll accept a life incognito.

I take a deep breath. Okay here goes nothing.

And here goes everything—my children's respect. And their trust. Maybe even their love.

Before I can get a word out, Jack walks over to her. He lays his arm on her shoulder. She looks up into his eyes, as if searching them for the answer she so desperately wants to hear.

But no. Even before he opens his mouth, I see the half-mast lids that warn of a rock-hard stance, the twitch of regret on the right side of his mouth.

He cannot accommodate. He can only commiserate. "Mary, please don't be mad at us because we can't tell you what you want to hear. Our mutual goal is that we all stay together. But if you'd prefer to go back to Hilldale, we will understand, and respect your wishes."

No, this isn't what Mary wants to hear.

Her acceptance comes with little fanfare. Hope fades from her eyes. A dull sadness takes its place. Her body seems slighter, as if it has shrunk along with the hope she had of getting her family home in one piece.

I don't blame her for freezing as Jack kisses her forehead, or for her hand going limp when I take it in mine.

Even when I squeeze it, it lays there, still and small.

When my hand drops away, her arm falls to her side. Like a sleepwalker, she turns and treads back to the couch. Since Rachel's death, it's become her cocoon.

When she flops onto it and crawls under the blanket, her foot touches something, and it tumbles to the floor.

It's a *Bloomsbury* script.

I scoop it up. "Mary, where did you get this?"

She peeks out from under the cover, but shrugs when she sees the script in my hand. "Sometimes Rachel and I would come here to read the scripts. I guess we forgot to return this one to Sebastian. Why? What's the big deal? I mean, now that they're both…gone." Her voice trails off.

"It's a very big deal. It may mean we can stay here in England, as opposed to going to Croatia."

The cover calls it out as Episode Two, from last season.

"Do you know if this is one of the scripts with the phrase that was changed?"

She takes it from my hand. After glancing at the first few pages, she says, "Yes, I think so." Slowly, she flips the pages. Finally, she stops and points to a bit of dialogue:

Virginia Woolf

Vanessa, we may not be as high-minded as the Clapham Sect, still I shudder to think we'll overlook the very same bourgeois habits we claim to abhor! All the more reason the group must address Duncan's latest indiscretion head on. It's a tangle, I know—but it cannot be ignored.

I pick up her iPad and log on to our Netflix account. *Bloomsbury* is prominent in our queue because Mary has viewed it so many times.

I fast-forward to this scene:

"…Vanessa, we may not be as high-minded as the Apostles, still I shudder—"

The website for *Bloomsbury* confirms that the episode aired exactly a week before an attempted suicide bombing in London.

It's all the proof we need to make our case to MI6.

Mary's eyes grow big. "I wouldn't mind staying here with you in England. Dad, do you think you can talk your bosses into it?"

Jack smiles. "Something tells me they'll approve it, yes."

"If that's the case, maybe another script will get us transferred back to the states." She rummages under the covers and pulls out another script—for the third episode in the upcoming season, which is to start next week.

Jack and I exchange glances. The script still to be aired may hold the key to a future attack.

He reaches for his cell phone and dials Arnie. "Are you in your room at the inn? …Great! We may have stumbled onto open source intel, and we'll need you to decode it for us, pronto...Arnie, are you there? ...Is everything okay? ... What? ...Don't go anywhere. We'll be right over."

We bury Mary in a hug between us.

This time, she doesn't pull away.

If only we could stay in this clinch forever.

But we can't. We're out the door again.

Maybe this time we won't have to run so far, or so fast.

I'VE NEVER SEEN ARNIE DRUNK.

It is not a pretty sight.

Jack holds up the two empty bottles of Guinness Stout. "How many ounces are in five hundred milliliters?"

"He's kind of busy here," I yell at him. I'm making sure Arnie doesn't fall into the toilet as he barfs into it.

"Approximately seventeen and a quarter ounces," Arnie rasps.

I've held many a head over a commode, but none that were cognizant enough to attempt math conversions. I guess that's what happens when you hang with frat boys from UCLA as opposed to MIT Comp Sci dropouts.

"Arnie, you've got to snap out of it! We need you, now more than ever." Jack lifts him up from under his armpits.

Wrong move. Arnie throws up again, only this time it's on Jack's brand new John Lobb brogues.

As Jack lets loose with gusto on some choice swear words, I aim Arnie back over the toilet and hold his head there until he stops heaving.

Finally, he raises his head again. "You don't understand. It's Emma! She's… she's…" he chokes on his words.

Or on whatever bile is crawling up his throat.

As he bends down over the commode to rid himself of it, I murmur, "Arnie, I know."

"What? You mean, she told you?" The puking stops, but hyperventilating takes its place.

Jack grabs a greasy, half-filled fish-and-chips bag, and empties its contents into a trash can. He hands it to Arnie, who takes deep breaths into it.

When Arnie pulls his face out of the bag, his cheeks and nose are covered in grease.

Now I think I'm going to barf. I swallow hard. "Emma felt she had to tell someone. She's so ashamed of herself." I pat his arm. "Arnie, she's worried about losing you."

He lifts his head, but he doesn't say anything. It will take a while before the color returns to his cheeks.

Or a smile to his lips.

He points to the scripts on the table. "I better get started."

Jack hesitates before picking them up. "Look, if you're not up to the task, we certainly understand. We can wait until tomorrow."

"No you can't. Donna's right. There's still a chance that Carl will recognize her from the camera footage. The sooner I decipher this intel, the quicker Ryan can backchannel it to his contacts at MI6, and the sooner you'll get your diplomatic immunity," he says, as he sticks out his hands.

Jack lays the scripts in them.

We've just reached the door when someone knocks. Jack

peeks out from a corner of the window's curtain before opening the door—

To Emma.

Seeing her, Arnie bends back over the toilet and heaves again.

This is too much for Emma. She tears up.

Worse yet, she runs to the trash can and throws up.

"Oh great," Jack mutters. "Now they're barfing in stereo."

We stand silently until both of them can sit upright again.

When they do, Emma whispers, "Arnie, I know you'll never forgive me for how stupid I was, or for what I've done. But I want you to know, from the bottom of my heart, that I didn't mean to hurt you, or to upset you, and that I'm ashamed of myself for falling for a pretty face when…when the love of my life has been right at my side, all along."

Arnie still can't look at her.

When she bows her head, her tears fall into her lap.

He can't see this. He can't hear this. But when exposed, the heart is an organ easily bruised.

Arnie's heart, however, was never really his. It always belonged to Emma, and hers to him.

So yes, he feels her heart breaking.

It is more than he can bear. This time when he heaves, it's to expel his grief, and to inhale the hope she extends his way.

This is obvious to me, and now to her, too, when he says, "I'll always love you, Emma. And I'll always be a part of your life, if you let me."

This is all she needs to hear to be at his side, to drop into his lap, and to kiss him as if it's the last kiss they'll share.

There will be so many more.

Jack's eye catches mine. He nods towards the door. As tender as this moment is for these two who we love and respect, the bottom line is that we are under the gun, figuratively and, perhaps soon, literally as well.

We've reached the door when Emma says, "Wait! Don't go! I came looking for you! I've got some really wonderful news!"

She slips her iPad out of her bag and beckons us over.

By the time we reach her side, what she wants us to see is already on her tablet's screen: the website admin panel for IslandOfMisfitSluts.com—the pornography website previously an asset of Breck Global Industries, which used to be owned by Babette Chiffray's first husband, Jonah, now deceased.

I stare at the screen. "Wasn't that site taken down after Chiffray's Global World Industries bought Breck's corporate holdings?"

"I thought so, too," Emma explains. "But then I did a little research and discovered it was spun off from the umbrella corporation prior to the sale of the trust." She pushes another button to open another page on the screen. "From what you can see in its Google analytics, the site is certainly thriving. Whoever owns it now is still making a ton of dough from it. Of course, the owner info is masked."

"Why is this important to us?" Jack asks.

"The site showcases thumbnail photos and fake profiles on the women held captive there. I scanned the faces until I found those of Antoinette and Serena, who were there in the bedroom with Breck the day he was killed. And guess what? The women are still featured!"

She clicks onto the thumbnail photo of Antoinette. Now I feel queasy. I still remember the look on her face when Carl put a bullet in her.

"I remembered Breck had video cameras set up in all the bedrooms of his compound on the island, so that he could record his sexual peccadillos with the women he held captive there, and those of his guests," Emma continues. "So I sifted through the video files and came up with this."

She opens a seemingly innocuous file labeled with a long string of numbers. Yes, there it is: the video footage of Jonah Breck's bedroom. In the clip, I enter it and raise a gun to Jonah, commanding him off the bed, where he's raping Antoinette. The camera picks up Carl, coming in behind me. I turn. He shoots—

But the bullet isn't for me. It hits Breck squarely in the forehead.

Carl's next bullet is for Antoinette.

"This clears you, Donna. Best yet, it implicates Carl," Jack murmurs. "We can go home now."

Arnie kisses Emma on the forehead. "Great work, little mama."

She frowns. "I think you can come up with a better nickname."

Arnie gets down on one knee. "How about Mrs. Locklear?"

Emma looks down at him. She is smiling through her tears.

She's also upchucking.

Ah, morning sickness! I remember you well.

Arnie's stomach can't take it. He joins in the fun.

Jack smiles. "They make beautiful music together, don't they?"

I nod. "Let's leave these two lovebirds alone."

"Jack, wait," Arnie gasps. "Before you leave, I've got a present for you, too."

He pulls a thumb drive from his pocket and tosses it to Jack.

"What is it?" I ask.

Arnie smiles. "Thanks to Jack's quick thinking this morning, it's just another nail in Carl's coffin—his admission to you, on the Metro, that he headed the Quorum."

Jack' turns to me. He's no longer smiling. "So, it was Carl you slipped out to meet, the night we were in DC."

I guess I've got some explaining to do.

"ALL THIS TIME, YOU KNEW I'D GONE OUT—BUT YOU NEVER asked me why?" Neither of us spoke the whole way back to our bungalow. But now that we are alone in our bedroom I'm doing my best to prove the theory that the best defense is a good defense.

"When you nudged me awake with your cold feet, I suspected you'd left the bed while I slept." The memory puts a slight smile on his face. "But I talked myself out of it. Then yesterday I remembered it was the same afternoon you got the text message you claimed was from Jeff, asking if he could stay up to watch the Broncos game. If he had called, he was lying to you because the Broncos were eliminated prior to the AFC playoffs."

I scowl. "And you would have said nothing, despite knowing he lied to his mother?"

"Jeff's shenanigans are harmless, compared to his mother's. If the Broncos were in the playoffs, he would have known it. On the other hand, considering your distaste for all things pigskin, I guessed—and rightly so—that you wouldn't." He shrugs. "If you were lying about the call, I felt I had a right to know why. I mean, it isn't as if you've 'fessed up in the meantime."

Guilty as charged.

I sit down next to him. "I was told to come alone. I had hoped to change Carl's mind about ruining Acme. As it turns out, I only made matters worse. Carl demanded the kids and I move to DC to be with him. Otherwise he'd fix it so that we'd both be tried for his terrorist crimes, and that Ryan and other Acme agents would also take the blame. I told him no, that I'd never leave you. He almost had me killed, but I escaped."

He takes my hand. "I'm sorry you went through that ordeal. But maybe some good will come out of it." He grins. "This morning I had the bright idea of asking Arnie to track the GPS coordinates for your cell that evening. He noticed it ended when you reached the L'Enfant Plaza Metro Station." He holds up the thumb drive. "Now that he's hacked the Metro's onboard webcam feed, I guess we'll be able to pass along verification of your account with our new president."

Jack inserts the thumb drive into his computer. While the

feed plays, he watches intently, but I have to avert my eyes when it gets to the part where Carl molests me.

When it ends, Jack forwards it to Ryan via a secure cloud, then turns off his computer.

I'm crying so hard when he takes me in his arms that I can't breathe. I start to hiccup.

"Hold your breath," he says, while patting me gently on the back.

I try, but my hiccups come fast and furious.

He kisses me, long and hard.

When we break apart, I sigh.

"See? It worked," he points out.

I pout. "I think they're coming back."

He laughs. "You're such a pretty little liar."

I stop his chuckle with a kiss of my own. "You know, you never need an excuse to kiss me."

He takes me at my word.

I take him to our bed.

I undress him slowly. I let him do the same to me.

I tremble under his touch. He grows larger under mine.

I never grow tired of the look of desire I see in his eyes, or the taste of his mouth, or the growl he releases as he enters me.

I crave the feeling of him inside me.

I live for these moments of shared ecstasy.

Afterward, as we lay in each other's arms, I know where my strength lies:

In him.

Carl should be very afraid.

17

The Wizard of Ahs

"Please, sir. We've done what you told us. We brought you the broomstick of the Wicked Witch of the West. We melted her!"

Judy Garland, as "Dorothy Gale" in The Wizard of Oz

THERE ARE A LOT OF WAYS IN WHICH MOVIES "GET IT WRONG." *For example:*

1. *Some change in detail slips past the continuity director. The job of this person is to make sure that everything in a particular scene—props, costumes, make-up, hair, lighting, sound—stays the same from take to take. For example, if the actor has a glass in her hand in one scene, but then it disappears after a cutaway to the close-up of someone else, this is a continuity mistake.*
2. *It includes an "anachronism"—something said, or*

shown, in the film did not exist during the time in which the film is set. A perfect example of this can be seen in the film, "Monuments Men." The American flag left flying at the mouth of a mine has fifty stars. In the year in which the story took place, there were only forty-eight states, and therefore only forty-eight stars.

3. *The film has a factual error. For example, in the movie "Gravity," scientists have pointed out some inaccuracies, including the fact that the tear rolling down actress Sandra Bullock's face would have never floated off because she was in zero gravity. It would have held onto her cheek due to surface tension.*

Ah, all the tiny little details that go into producing a movie! No wonder you'd rather watch one than make one.

Besides, you were born to be a critic. Just ask your children.

Lee Chiffray's secretary, Eileen Woodley, assures us the president will be seeing us any moment now. He has only kept Jack, Ryan, and me waiting twenty minutes, which I guess is a good sign, since those being ushered out now are two five-star generals. I recognize them as the heads of the NSA and INR. Both were former clients of Acme, and who have the utmost respect for Ryan.

Or, I should say, had. They scan our faces and then move on.

Lee has taken well to his new digs in the West Wing.

Pictures of his new wife and stepdaughter, Babette and Janie, adorn the credenza behind his desk.

Lee moves out from behind his massive desk to shake Ryan's hand, and Jack's. I earn a long, adoring glance and a peck on the cheek.

Yes, Jack notices this. His gaze shifts between Lee and me. I wink to signal, *no worries! Just being neighborly!*

Jack knows differently. Lee and I have a history, sort of. He tried to buy me when I was sold into slavery, on Fantasy Island.

I guess he thought it was the right thing to do. Sure beats mowing a lawn or dropping off a casserole.

I still believe Lee did it in order to buy my freedom, not to keep me as a pet, or a sex slave or anything.

Even before he was POTUS, Lee was considered a catch: as the founder and CEO of Global World Industries, he's one of the wealthiest men on the planet. While Lee is president, his assets are being held in a blind trust.

Jack has held the belief that GWI is somehow entwined with the Quorum, but he hasn't been able to verify this. Frankly, I think he's barking up the wrong tree.

Maybe I just wish that were the case. If Jack's right, the branches of that tree now reach into the White House.

No matter our past, after today's meeting, I presume Lee and I also have a future together, although at this very moment, I don't know exactly what that means.

I guess I'll soon find out.

He ushers us toward the two large couches in the room, which sit opposite each other. An aide places a coffee service on the table between us. Since we've been told we're only to have, at the most, fifteen minutes of the president's time, I take this as a good sign. *Come on in, set a spell.*

Ryan must think differently, because he refuses a cuppa joe in a cup embossed with the presidential seal. "Thank you for taking the time to meet with us, Mr. President. I don't know if you've had time to review the dossier I forwarded to you."

Lee nods. "In fact, I have. And I agree with Acme's findings that make an irrefutable case for Jack and Donna to be dropped from the international terrorists list, as well as for Acme's reinstatement as an approved vendor with the US intelligence community."

"I can imagine Director Stone isn't pleased with your decision." I detect a shadow of a smile on Ryan's lips. He is relieved to get back the thing that matters most to him: his honor.

"He'll learn to live with it. More to the point, he knows better than to question it." I presume Lee's grimace is a reflection of his argument with Carl over us. Lee's been in office less than two months, and yet, already, he looks older than his forty-six years.

Jack leans forward. "We hope you think the other intel we've collected from various Quorum hot spots also makes a case for the removal of Carl Stone as DI. Having a known terrorist in your administration will throw the country into chaos, and put our citizens and our national security in harm's way."

Lee shrugs. "Based on what I've seen, I can understand why you'd feel this way. But Acme's allegations have yet to be substantiated, despite the CIA's attempts to do so."

"It's no longer just our word against his, Mr. President," I point out. "Have you reached out to the eye witnesses who were there when Carl committed these atrocities? They can verify our reports."

"Our agents in those countries have tried. But your sources are now either deceased or have disappeared." He pulls out the pictures of our witnesses, taken from our video interviews. He points to the one of Roger Cavanaugh. "Mr. Cavanaugh broke his neck while fox hunting."

A wave of guilt washes over me as I remember running into Sebastian on the morning he met Jack and me at the Railway Inn. Now I realize he hadn't known Roger at all, but tricked me into dropping his name so that the Quorum could get to him.

Lee frowns as he stares down at the photo of Serena. "And Ms. La Costa, her husband and infant baby were killed by one of the Venezuelan paramilitary *colectivos* in one of their door-to-door roundups, just last night."

"What? But—that can't be true!" Abu arranged for a private jet to pick them up tonight, in fact.

The guilt hits me: *we should have pulled them out sooner.*

Ryan catches my eye as if to say, *get ahold of yourself.* To change the subject, he says, "I wish that were the case. And, unfortunately, I have more bad news. The Quorum operative you chased down in France, Mr. Weber, has disappeared from his estate. No one has seen him—or any of his staff, for that matter—for the past three days. The place sits empty."

Jack looks over at me. I know what he's thinking: *He played us.*

"Who is he, exactly?" Lee asks, frowning.

"Carl's original handler in the Quorum," Jack explains.

"In other words, there are no eye witnesses to validate your accusations. That being said, Carl Stone stays in his position as Director of Intelligence." Lee's tone says it all: *case closed.*

"Despite all you see before you?" Jack asks. "Even the part where the new Director of Intelligence molests Donna on the Metro, then admits to several terrorist acts, and threatens to throw innocent people in jail for his own treasonous acts if she doesn't kowtow to his blackmail?"

I'm about to say something, but Ryan catches my eye. He knows I'm embarrassed by Jack's outburst.

Jack ignores my frown, though, as he waits for Lee's answer.

Lee pauses before giving it. His tone is not defensive, or an angry one. His words are cautious. "The web feed you provided me also showed Mrs. Stone holding a knife to her husband's neck, leading me to believe she is quite capable of taking care of herself. Their mutual dislike and anger issues aside, for various reasons Mr. Stone will stay in his current position. But, thank you, for your concern." Lee rises.

Talk about a broad hint.

We all stand. When Jack puts out his hand, Lee takes it. "Mr. President, whatever he has on you, we can take care of it."

"Acme's plate will be kept quite full, believe me." From the sadness in his eyes, I don't doubt that in the least. "Nonetheless, I appreciate your concern."

When he turns to say goodbye to me, it's with a slight

bow. No handshake, no peck on the cheek. Our mutual admiration society is officially over.

At least as far as I'm concerned.

None of us speaks during the long walk through the West Wing, and back out onto Pennsylvania Avenue. I'm sure Ryan is thinking of all the work that will be needed to put the office back together. Jack is angry and frustrated because, once again, Carl has slipped through our grasp.

As for me, I'll be relieved to get home.

Well to Hilldale, anyway. Where we'll live while we're rebuilding our house will be a whole other matter.

I wonder how Dominic will feel about hosting us? We had to put up with his lordly airs when he stayed as a guest in our home, while his was being renovated. It's time he returned the favor.

I don't know who to feel sorrier for—him because he'll be in a constant state of worry over the proximity of the children to his antiques, or the kids, for having to tiptoe through that mausoleum he calls a home.

I'll make it up to him with my cooking. He'll grouse about getting love handles, even as he takes third helpings.

At the same time, I'll worry about the number of martinis I'll be downing during what Dominic calls "tea time," but hey, playing bartender is one of the few things he does very well.

Just like old times—when we thought Carl was dead and buried.

If only that were the case.

18

Heaven Can Wait

"The likelihood of one individual being right increases in direct proportion to the intensity with which others are trying to prove him wrong."

James Mason, as "Mr. Jordan"

DON'T BELIEVE EVERYTHING YOU SEE ON THE SCREEN. FROM PLOT and dialogue to location and lip lock, it's all an illusion, meant to transport you out of the here-and now, into a wish-I-were-there fantasy. Here are three perfect examples:

- *Example #1: The stars aren't really as pretty as they look on the big screen. Spend just twenty minutes in a make-up trailer and you'll realize that the dewy skin on your favorite actress isn't God's gift to her, but a touch-up with an airbrush brandished by the skilled hands of*

*the make-up artist she has written into every film
contract she's ever signed.*

You too deserve your own on-call make-up artist, who will keep
you ready for your close-ups for all the many soirees on your calen-
dar. It would behoove you to keep such a person on retainer, even if
it means whittling down your child's college tuition account to pay
his fee. Better yet, send your child to beauty school, and you've
killed two birds with one stone!

- *Example #2: The sets are never as intricate, or as
  humongous as you'd imagine. Sometimes the furniture
  is the weight of kindling, and the sets are no more than
  well-painted cardboard flats. At other times, you're
  looking at computer-generated imagery (CGI), which
  means the actors are emoting in front of a large flat
  green screen.*

You might also consider a CGI stage as your living room! By
filling it with various photos, you can change your furnishings as
quickly and as often as you like. And since it doesn't really exist, it
will be so much easier to clean.

- *Example #3: Actors may have great chemistry on
  screen, but that doesn't mean they even like each other
  once the director calls out, "Cut!" Sure, they seem to be
  all hot and heavy with each other when the cameras are
  rolling, but more than likely she's holding her breath
  because of his bad breath, and he's thinking about the
  real love of his life—his boyfriend.*

In other words, the man at your side is the true happily ever after in your life, so give him a big meaningful kiss—

But first, pop a breath mint. Illusions in the real world have to be done on a budget.

THE VERANDA OF CHATEAU FLEMING—DOMINIC'S NICKNAME for his Hilldale mini-mansion—encircles the whole house, providing shade in the hot Southern California sun at all times. I've been out here since sunrise staring out at the hills that encircle our little hamlet…I've been out here for so long that my cup of coffee is already cold.

That's perfectly fine by me, even if it is cause for concern to Dominic's valet, Giles, who hovers just out of view in case I come to my senses and actually demand a spot o' hot.

As tempting as Willow's Malibu place is to Jack and me, while school is in session, the kids would much rather hang here, so Dominic is crashing there.

In fact, he's taken Willow up on her offer to train her in martial arts. I have a feeling she's got a few tricks up her sleeve he'll appreciate, too. Hopefully they will have changed the sheets before we're ready to check it out for ourselves.

Lee Chiffray was good to his word. Acme is flooded with work. Both Dominic and Jack are on overnight assignments.

I've begged off since Jack and I have been home, which is going on two weeks now. I love doing nothing. Let others take on the weight of the world. I am perfectly content to get back to my baking and gardening. Perhaps I'll take up knitting and scrapbooking, too—

Oh, who in hell am I kidding?

Pakistan is in turmoil. The Middle East is a boiling pot. China is the US financial markets' puppet master—

Doesn't anyone give a damn?

And to top it all off, the Hilldale Elementary School auction still needs its big get-everyone-to-bust-out-of-their-Spanx item: dinner at the "Western White House," which is what the media has dubbed Lion's Lair, Lee and Babette's eighty-six-room palace on the hill.

Snore.

Both happen to be back in Hilldale. In fact, according to the *Los Angeles Times,* Lee is using his birthday as an excuse for a four-day weekend.

To justify the time off, he's meeting with a few international dignitaries and attending a fundraiser or two.

Which reminds me: I'm to meet with Miss Darling in half an hour. As the elementary school's auction chairman, I'm to give her an update on auction item donations and ticket sales, both of which have been lethargic, at best. Apparently I've yet to be embraced by the yummy mommies who run Trisha's school.

Or maybe my reputation precedes me—not as described in my rap sheet that can be found on the FBI's Most Wanted list, but by what is whispered by Cheever's mother, Penelope, and the rest of her middle school posse.

Poor Miss Darling. If she had turned me in back then, she'd have the reward money, and the school would never have to do another auction again.

All the more reason this event has to be a success.

I force myself out of the settee and head out the door.

Miss Darling waits until we've gone over all the logistical details of the event before she asks, "So, have you followed up yet on asking the Chiffrays about the auction prize?"

How do I break the news to her that I no longer have, or want, anything to do with Lee?

For my own wellbeing, I have to let her down. "Sorry, no can do," I tell her.

"But Trisha and Janie are the closest of friends," she murmurs.

"Yes, well, that's true for the girls, but Babette and I have never been close."

"I know for a fact that President Chiffray remembers the school quite fondly," she counters.

She's right. He's already sent a hefty donation for the math and science fund.

She smiles knowingly. "And he thinks fondly of you too, I might add."

I can feel the heat crawling up my neck. I force myself to smile. "Miss Darling, were you to ask Babette directly—or the president, for that matter—I'm sure you'd get the gift."

"That's the whole point. I've sent a handwritten letter already, to both of the Chiffrays." She sighs. "But I'm getting nowhere." She shakes her head sadly. "They both know you, and they know you're chairing this event.

Wouldn't they be offended if you didn't reach out to them?"

She's got a point.

What do I have to be afraid of, anyway? For one thing, Lee owes me.

I nod. "Okay, I'll see if either of them will take my call." I fumble for my car key. "But please don't be too disappointed if I also hit a brick wall."

She pats my arm. "Donna, I can tell you already that you won't. You're one of the most diligent parents I know."

I wish I had her confidence in me.

More importantly, I wish I had her confidence in Lee Chiffray.

Here's hoping he doesn't disappoint Miss Darling as much as he's disappointed me.

19

All the President's (Wo)men

"It involves the entire U.S. Intelligence Community. FBI… CIA…Justice…it's incredible. …It was mainly to protect the covert operations. It leads everywhere. Get out your notebook. There's more. Your lives are in danger."

Hal Holbrook, as "Deep Throat" in All the President's Men

IS YOUR HEART PALPITATING BECAUSE YOU'RE *THIS CLOSE* TO *one of your favorite actors of all time? Here are some quick etiquette tips in the art of the autograph:*

- *Tip #1: Don't ask if you're in a lavatory of any nature. It doesn't matter if it's the restroom at the Ritz, the Staples Center or the Oscars, one of you will be doing something the other won't want to see or hear—let alone come in contact with a pen or paper from the other, while doing so.*

- *Tip #2: Don't ask if you're on the movie set with him and he's going through his actor's prep in order to get into character—especially if he's a serial killer, because you're giving him the perfect reason to wring your neck.*
- *Tip #3: Don't ask if he's in an argument with his significant other. However, if it leads to a break-up and the actor is looking for a shoulder to cry on, bare yours —or better, your chest—and hand him a pen.*

"YES, THE PRESIDENT HAS BEEN EXPECTING YOU," EILEEN Woodley replies crisply, when I call to make an appointment. "In fact, he's asked me to block out a half-hour, starting at four o'clock today."

He's expecting me? How audacious is that?

The manners drilled into me by mother come to mind. *Always a lady, even under pressure. You catch more flies with honey than vinegar.*

In this case, my father's lessons also apply: *Keep your gun cocked and loaded—but don't fire until you see the whites of their eyes.*

Figuratively speaking, of course.

"I'll be sure to be prompt. I know he keeps a pretty tight business schedule," I say sweetly, then hang up.

I win at this war of misplaced trust if I get him to agree to the auction prize. I lose if I show anger.

My greatest weapon is my indifference.

WHEN I ARRIVE, I'M SHOWN INTO THE STUDY. HE DOESN'T KEEP me waiting long. California agrees with him. He's only been here two days, but apparently, it's been long enough for him to acquire a healthy tan. The presidency has put enough gray in his naturally dark hair that it is now light enough to pass for sun-bleached hair. His surfer boy good looks roll back his age once again and belie his position as leader of the free world.

Ken and Barbie are both living in the White House.

All weekend, photographers have been standing on the sidewalk flanking the fence around Lion's Lair's private golf course, a nine-hole course. They are still far enough away that they have cameras with telephoto lenses to capture his perfect golf swing, and the admiring glances of foreign dignitaries and the business movers-and-shakers who make up each day's foursome.

One of today's players is the Yemeni president. I still cringe at the memory of my role in the theft of his country's greatest antiquity.

Thank goodness that little caper will never get out. Being the cause of an international incident? I could likely kiss my pardon adios! Or in this case, *ma`a as-salāma.*

Lee is all smiles as he walks into the room. When he comes over to greet me, he leans in so that our faces are close enough for a friendly kiss. I counter his move by leaning back, offering my hand instead.

When our eyes meet, I see the disappointment in his.

That's okay. This is one emotional minuet I'll be sitting out. My dance card is full, thank you very much.

"Welcome home, Mr. President."

Hearing the sincerity in my voice, his shoulders relax a bit. "Thank you, Donna. You're the perfect welcoming committee."

Why should he be nervous? It's I who comes, wide-brimmed straw hat in hand. It's a pale yellow, and matches my favorite yellow polka-dot dress.

"I hope Babette and Janie are well. I'm sure Trisha will be happy to see Janie, if it can be arranged before you head East again." *I don't like the way he's staring at me, as if I'm the one who got away.*

Well, I guess I did, thanks to him.

"You look like spring," he says finally.

"It's always spring in Orange County," I counter.

"You love taunting me, don't you?" His flirtatiousness is delivered with a raised brow.

"I wouldn't dare," I murmur. "I may end up in jail."

His smile fades. "That's not fair, Donna."

I shrug. "You're right. It wasn't. I've got the presidential pardon to prove it."

"And yet, you still don't forgive me."

"If you say yes to the auction gift of a dinner here, with the winner, we'll call it even. Agreed?"

He laughs. "You're on—as long as you rig it so that you win." He motions me to sit on the settee by the fireplace.

Instead of taking the chair beside it, he eases in beside me.

He's taking me at my word. He's been getting off easy all his life. Why should this be any exception?

"The school will write in any contingencies to the gift. I'm sure the winners would appreciate a photo taken with you and the First Lady—"

"Whatever you want. You can arrange the details with Eileen." He doesn't rise. He's not acting like the Commander-in-Chief.

"But of course. Well, thank you again for your generosity to the school—"

"I owe you an apology," he interrupts bluntly. "You're right. Carl is a terrorist, and needs to be locked up."

Duh, yeah.

"Explain to me, then, Mr. President, why did you champion him for the directorship?"

"You know, you can call me Lee in private."

"But…it's no longer proper that I do so."

"You're right, Mrs. Stone. It isn't. However, if you keep talking to me as if I'm some sort of statue, I'll know I've lost your friendship."

Is that what we are, friends?

Should I need to ask, it's proof he's right.

With Carl sitting in high cotton, I need all the friends I can get—especially this one.

"No—Lee, you haven't lost it." I take a deep breath. "Now, answer my question."

He looks away for a moment. When our eyes meet again, the dread I see in his face makes me so sad. "I met Carl during the negotiations for Global World Industries' purchase of Breck Industries. As the executor of Jonah's trust, he negotiated the deal on Babette's behalf."

"I see. Go on."

"As you know better than anyone, Jonah's participation in the Quorum was covered up from the public. The only knowledge I had of the entity known as the Quorum was through its joint ventures with Breck Industries. One of those ventures was Fantasy Island. I found out later it was Jonah's personal playground."

I snicker. "Oh, it was more than that."

"Yes, when the time was right—that is, when he knew it would ruin GWI should the word get out—Carl took great joy in revealing its original name—Misfit Quay, and the fact that Jonah's porn site, The Island of Misfit Sluts, was run from there, as well as the fact that the women he used were slaves, and snuffed out." He shakes his head angrily. "I was able to convince him to use the island for legitimate purposes. GWI agreed to underwrite Fantasy Island for Boarke. What we didn't know is that the Quorum was paying him to house political prisoners in the basement of the Hunt Club, right there on the island."

"When did you find out Boarke was using the prisoners as human prey?"

He shrugs. "I guess I found out around the same time you did—while I was vacationing there with Babette. I found it odd that one of our pilots had disappeared. Battoo led me in the right direction." He turns to face me. "It was a nightmare of an investment for GWI. To find out the true purpose of the resort—"

"Including the Quorum's goal of testing a lethal plague

virus on the prisoners?"

He nods. "Yes, that, too."

Suddenly, I remember Trisha spelling the word Quorum —something she claims she learned from Babette. "Lee, I have to ask you: do you think Babette knows the true mission of the Quorum?"

He slumps into the settee. "I…can't answer that. She knew Jonah was a member of 'some silly private little men's club,' as she put it. And she met Carl through it. She saw him climb up its ranks, from part of the security detail to a full-fledged member."

"You were close to Catherine Martin, were you not?"

"Originally, she was a friend of the Brecks."

"Carl killed her husband, Robert. You read that in our report."

"With what I know of him now, I have no reason to doubt you on that. But if you remember, the webcam video Acme provided, in which Catherine and the shooter discuss Robert's assassination, didn't show a clear picture of the man's face. To top it off, his voice was electronically altered. Considering your history with Carl, further substantiation would be needed, and Catherine won't validate his participation."

Of course not. She's afraid of Carl's wrath, and in prison, she's a sitting duck.

"Whose idea was it for you to be Catherine's running mate?"

"It came from Catherine. Of course, Babette was excited, and nudged me into accepting." He shrugs. "I'd be lying if I didn't admit that my ego had something to do with it, too."

"And, of course, Carl encouraged you."

He nods.

"The Quorum was funneling cash to Catherine. She was bought and paid for. Then, when Carl learned Robert was going to divorce her right in the middle of the election, he convinced Catherine that Robert had to be exterminated; it gave him one more thing to hold over her head. It also gave him the nomination as Director of Intelligence."

I look him in the eye. "But you were Carl's failsafe. Should she implode before, during, or after the election, he needed someone in place to carry on with the nomination. He needed to control the vice president, too." I take his hand in mine. "Lee, what does Carl have on you?"

He rises in order to pace the floor.

When he stops, it's directly in front of me. "He knows I killed a young woman. Her death was accidental, but Carl, of course, can make it look otherwise." He crouches in front of me, his head bowed. "He knows the woman and I had a daughter together, and he knows where the girl is." He's choking up now, and I can barely hear him. "He knew of my connection to Catherine and Robert Martin and he encouraged Babette and me to be Congresswoman Martin's biggest supporters in the presidential primaries. Carl made it seem that it was Catherine's idea that she make me her running mate: just your average Joe from Kansas, who parlays a small Canadian tech start-up into a successful international conglomerate. A match made in heaven, right? Later, of course, I learned that it was Carl's idea all along. So yes, you're right. I was his Trojan horse into the oval office. If I didn't make him DI, he could have easily ruined me."

I stroke his head, but I doubt I'm giving him much comfort.

Finally, he lifts his head. He takes my hand. "You are my greatest weapon against Carl."

And he is mine. We both know it.

"GWI funded Addison's movie, didn't it?"

"Yes," he confesses quietly. "It's why Acme was called in as consultants. I told Addison to pay you whatever it took to get you."

"You mean, we were being overpaid on purpose?" I have to laugh at this. "You've just burst my bubble! It was the easiest money I've ever made, and certainly less dangerous than covert ops—well, except when there's a murderer on the set."

"I also made sure that the shooting locations were close enough for you to get to the witnesses you needed. Ryan back-channeled the necessary cities," he reminds me.

I shake my head. "I thought it was too much of a coincidence."

"If I was going to clear you of Carl's charges, I needed someone with a vested interest to do the legwork. I couldn't jeopardize anyone who worked under Carl. You were already on the run. And besides, you knew where all the bodies were buried, literally."

"So, where does this leave us, Lee?"

"Acme has the same priority it always had—take down the Quorum, and Carl. Only now, you report only to me. I'll make sure you have every resource you need at your fingertips."

"Works for me." We shake on it.

That's when I see it, displayed in a glass case on one of the wall-to-ceiling bookcases flanking the fireplace—

The Queen of Sheba's scepter.

Lee follows my gaze. "Ah, the scepter! Like it?"

I nod slowly. "You bet. May I get a closer look?"

"Of course." He walks me over. Slowly he opens the top of the display case, and pulls it out for me to examine.

Yes, it's the real thing.

"Lee, where did you get this?"

"Babette gave it to me, last night. As an early birthday gift."

"Isn't one of your guests the Yemeni president?"

"Yes, that's right."

"I presume he hasn't seen it."

"No. This is my private office. I rarely bring anyone here."

"Good. Don't—at least not him, especially while you have this in your possession, unless you don't mind re-gifting."

He frowns. "Why would I do that?"

"Because it was stolen from his country a few weeks ago."

"How could that be? Babette said she bought it from a reputable antiquities broker!" He takes a closer look. "Are you sure?"

I nod.

"How do you know?"

Gulp. "Don't ask. But I would strongly suggest you honor him with its return. Think of it as a great photo op, and an even stronger tie to one of the wealthiest nations in the Arab Emirates."

He laughs, "I'm sure Babette will be disappointed. For saving me from my first international incident, I'd like to invite you and Jack to my birthday celebration dinner tonight. I'll personally introduce you to our honored guests." He frowns. "And one who is not so honored. Carl will be here, too, along with some other IC directors."

"Lucky you. Seriously, Lee, I think I'll pass."

He takes my hand. "Please don't, Donna. I wouldn't mind rattling his cage. It's a good strategy."

He's got a point.

"And besides, I'd enjoy having another beautiful woman at the table."

"Oh, is Donna joining us?" Lee and I look up to find Babette at the door.

Lee forces a smile. "Both the Stones, in fact."

"You mean all three of them, don't you? We can't forget your new Director of Intelligence." I don't know if her brittle smirk is meant for Lee or me.

Not that it matters. I shake Lee's hand.

This time, when he leans forward to kiss my cheek, I don't pull away.

"I'll walk Donna out," Babette murmurs.

Our stroll down the long hallway is silent almost to the grand foyer's front door. There is no small talk. The battalion of Secret Service personnel we pass are as still as the furniture. But when we reach the front door, she turns to me. "I know your game plan, Donna. And I can tell you to forget it. Lee is leading you on."

I glare at her. "You don't know what you're talking about. Seriously, Babette, there's no reason to be jealous—"

"Wait—are you being serious? Do you really think I'm jealous?" Her laughter rings through the foyer's two-story rotunda. "Poor Donna! You really are as naïve as Carl says you are!"

"I don't know what you mean by that. The last thing my husband would call me is naïve."

"I don't mean *Jack*, dear. We can all call him that now, can't we?" she smirks.

"I hadn't realized you're so close to *Carl*," I throw back at her.

"We are. In fact, he's found me a wonderful shoulder to lean on during this whole ordeal of false accusations." She narrows her eyes. "I know the whole story."

"No, you just know his side of it."

"The only thing that matters is being on the *winning* side."

"You're the First Lady, Babette. It doesn't get better than that."

She shrugs. "I'm never satisfied. It's the cross I bear."

I'd like to personally nail her to it, but I only got one get-out-of-jail card and I've already used it, so instead I start the long trek home.

I come home to Dominic's to find the front door open. Giles is nowhere to be seen.

"Mary?" I call out. "Jeff? Trisha?"

"We're in here, Mom!" Jeff calls out.

Not good. His voice is coming from Dominic's grand salon—a room he has specifically requested stay free of kiddie cooties.

I walk toward it. "What are you doing in there? You know Mr. Fleming's house rules! In the kitchen—*now*! I'd like your help getting dinner ready for you. Your father and I will be eating out tonight."

"Are we?" Carl stands in the doorway of the salon. He is holding Trisha's hand.

No.

No, please. Not now, and not this way.

"Mommy, are you okay?" Trisha runs toward me.

I take her in my arms and hold her tight.

He will never touch her again. I'll make sure of that.

Mary and Jeff come running up as well. Neither of them is smiling.

"Mary, you and Jeff can start dinner. Take Trisha with you." They recognize the tone in my voice. It tells them all they need to know: *I'm not happy with what I see before me.*

They practically run down the hall toward the kitchen, nearly knocking over Giles, who has stepped out of the library. The tray in his hand totters precariously for a moment. Ice tinkles against glass, and glass trembles against sterling silver. "The gentleman's libation," Giles murmurs.

Carl smiles. "Thank you, my good man."

But before he can reach for it, I snatch it up and belt it down. "Party's over," I snarl at Carl. "Get the hell out of here."

"Shhhh," he warns me. "We mustn't fight in front of the children."

I point toward the front door. "Get out—now!"

"What? No niceties at all? What happened to the gracious wife who used to greet me with a drink in hand, a gourmet meal on the table, and wearing one of those cute little sundresses accessorized with a pearl necklace"—He gives me the once-over—"you know, like this yellow polka-dotted number. Isn't it the one you wore when you met with our old pal, Serena La Costa? I also like dainty housecoats, like that pink one you wore when you visited my old pal, Eric Weber."

His remarks bring on a cold dread that makes me shudder. "I know you had your people kill her. If you're saying you found her through me—"

"Read my lips, dear wife—yes, you were indeed the hound who sniffed out that pretty little fox. Sebastian planted a GPS bug on your dress so that the Quorum could trace your whereabouts while you traipsed through the 'burbs of *la ciudad capital*." He pauses in thought. "Hey with your new connections, here's something you can pitch Hollywood—'The Housewives of Caracas.'" He pumps the air with his fist. "*Viva la revolución bonita, sí?*"

He asked for it. A moment later, I have my Glock between his legs—pointed upward. "Why are you here, Carl? Answer quickly, unless the thought of being eunuch appeals to you. It would certainly put a smile on my face."

He winces. "You're on the guest list so you should know why—the big shindig over at the POTUS palace, for Lee's birthday. Hey, maybe we'll be lucky and it'll be dinner and a show! What are the chances they'll play some footage from your—*our* biopic? At least the good part—you know, where you almost get washed out to sea."

I tap him with my gun to remind him he's taking a chance with the family jewels.

He nods. "You're right. The odds are slim to none. That's okay. I hear the book is much better. Perhaps you'll let me read it some time—or at least the sexy parts—which I presume are all your scenes with me, because I'm sure Jack's a snore in the sack."

I guess Sebastian told him about my diaries after all.

Oh...*shit*.

I blush at the thought. "Not on your life, or mine for that matter." Time to change the subject, and quick. "Carl, what I'm asking you is how long you've been *in here—in this house.*"

"Long enough to introduce myself to my children."

"You mean—you told them?"

He shrugs. "Was I supposed to wait the rest of my life for you to do it?"

"No! ...I mean, yes! ... I mean..." I take a deep breath. "It was up to me to tell them!"

He looks down at me. His eyes hold no sympathy for me. Only pity.

"Then do it, Donna. Or I'll have to."

I let his arm drop.

He's right about one thing. Maybe it's time.

He straightens his jacket as he walks away.

I stumble back into the house. I take my time walking to the kitchen. The children have a pot boiling on Dominic's state-of-the-art Wolfe range. Mary is cutting up a green pepper, I presume for spaghetti sauce. She stops, though, when she sees me. "You can put the bag of noodles in now," she commands Jeff.

He nods, but he's got his eyes on me, too. He wonders why I reacted the way I did to the stranger who seemed so friendly.

Mary grabs my arm and walks me back down the hall. "Mom, wasn't he the man I met when the Russian president was here?"

I nod, but the lump in my throat is too big for me to speak.

"I remember he has the same name as us—Stone. But, who is he?"

I swallow hard. This is the moment I've dreaded since I found out the truth about Carl.

Right here, right now.

I open my mouth, but the words don't come out.

As it turns out, it doesn't matter because Mary isn't listening to me, anyway.

Instead, she's running into Jack's arms.

So are Jeff and Trisha. "Daddy is home," Trisha squeals.

They've missed him terribly. They always do when he is gone longer than a night or two.

I guess it brings back the memories of all the years they had without a father.

But no one could be sadder about life without Jack than me.

He takes us all in his arms—Mary, Trisha, Jeff, and of course, me too. The group hug is tight and warm.

It is the sweetest moment, one I will cherish forever.

Yes, their father is home.

The children are the first to break away. They are hungry, and by now, the noodles have turned to mush, anyway.

The girls back down the hall, toward the kitchen. Jeff starts after them, but then stops to ask, "Can we order a pizza instead?"

"Yes," I answer.

He rewards me with a fist pump. "Yeah! Pizza night!"

Then I lose myself in Jack's bear hug, and in his kiss, and in his murmurs of how much he's missed me.

I hush him as he mutters about his surprise at seeing Carl drive away from the house, and through his vow that he'll kill Carl if he so much as laid a finger on any of us.

"Kill him anyway," I laugh through my tears.

Does he know I'm kidding?

For now, anyway.

Still, I reassure him Carl swore to leave it up to me to tell them the truth.

Not today, but soon.

Jack pulls away slightly, but still he won't let me go. "The truth? That's easy. The truth is that I'm their father."

Yes, it is the truth. Enough said.

We go inside so that I can call Eileen and send our regrets, for the most important reason of all:

It's pizza night, and my children's father has come home.

—*THE END*—

Other Books by Josie Brown

The True Hollywood Lies Series

Hollywood Hunk

Hollywood Whore

The Totlandia Series

The Onesies - Book 1 (Fall)

The Onesies - Book 2 (Winter)

The Onesies - Book 3 (Spring)

The Onesies - Book 4 (Summer)

The Twosies - Book 5 (Fall)

The Twosies – Book 6 (Winter)

The Twosies - Book 7 (Spring)

The Twosies - Book 8 (Summer)

More Josie Brown Novels

The Candidate

Secret Lives of Husbands and Wives

The Baby Planner

How to Reach Josie

To write Josie, go to:
mailfromjosie@gmail.com

To find out more about Josie, or to get on her eLetter list for
book launch announcements, go to her website:
www.JosieBrown.com

You can also find her at:

www.AuthorProvocateur.com

twitter.com / JosieBrownCA

facebook.com / josiebrownauthor

pinterest.com / josiebrownca

instagram.com / josiebrownnovels

www.ingramcontent.com/pod-product-compliance
Lightning Source LLC
Chambersburg PA
CBHW070606170726
48291CB00003B/719